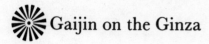 Gaijin on the Ginza

James Kirkup

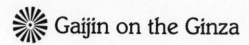 Gaijin on the Ginza

A Novel

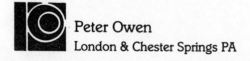 Peter Owen
London & Chester Springs PA

PETER OWEN PUBLISHERS
73 Kenway Road London SW5 0RE
Peter Owen books are distributed in the USA by
Dufour Editions Inc. Chester Springs PA 19425–0449

First published in Great Britain 1991
© James Kirkup 1991

British Library Cataloguing in Publication Data
Kirkup, James *1918–*
  Gaijin on the Ginza.
  I. Title
  823.914 [F]

  ISBN 0–7206–0833–3

Printed in Great Britain by Billings of Worcester

To Sachiko and Ken-chan,
and in memory of
their mother, Mariko,
with admiration and love

Everest, Jimi

✻ Foreword: A Comic Love–Hate Relation

✻ *Gaijin on the Ginza* is a work of fiction. But it is based on a certain important aspect of reality in contemporary Japan which tourists and businessmen and other short-time visitors never see. Their brief encounters with the Japanese and with the Japan of the Japanese Tourist Board travel posters and luxuriously illustrated coffee-table books often leave them ecstatic about the refinement, politeness, kindness and honesty of their hosts. All that is true enough. Yet there is another, mysterious, darker, more impenetrable side to Japanese life, to everyday existence, which can be glimpsed only after years of residence, of working and playing with the Japanese.

Gaijin means 'outsider'. It refers to all those who, whatever their degree of integration into Japanese society and culture, will always be non-Japanese and therefore aliens. Foreigners residing in Japan are subjected to various forms of bureaucratic and police surveillance. Such control is discreet, but the longer one lives in Japan the more one becomes aware of its all-pervasive, mysterious workings. Only recently has the word 'aliens' been removed from notices at immigration offices and at airports, and replaced by 'non-Japanese'. Yet one always has to carry one's alien registration card, for one can be stopped at any moment by the police and asked to show it. At such traumatic moments it is best to forget whatever Japanese one knows. If one has come out without that card, one is escorted to the nearest police-box or station until one's identity can be confirmed. Then one has to write a formal letter of apology to the police, in Japanese of course. (Since childhood, I have always felt I am an alien, even in my own country. I am an artist in alienation, and that skill helped me in Japan.) Such controls are a small price to pay for the pains and pleasures of living in Japan. We are far from the unhappy days of the dread *kempeitai* or 'thought police'. Nevertheless, for the average Westerner from a democratic country, there remains the distinct sense or vague apprehension that one is living in a police state. And it is a state controlled also by the Japanese themselves, always eager

7

to denounce foreign ways they may consider criminal, subversive or simply 'different'. The Japanese terror of the *qu'en dira-t-on?* or 'what will the neighbours say?' acts in a subtle but efficiently repressive way to keep people in line. Japan is a self-policing society. That is why foreigners say there is so little crime.

This state of things has been getting worse in recent times, with the renewed self-confidence of the 'economic miracle' bolstering the just pride of the Japanese in their remarkable achievements. No longer are blond, blue-eyed foreigners looked upon with awe and envy. The modern Japanese has seen the world and made deductions from which he arrives at the conclusion that Japan is best, and *gaijin* are more than ever aliens, amusing entertainers at best, and never to be taken very seriously.

It is against this background that I have set the characters of my novel – both 'aliens' and 'natives'. It shows the often precarious existence led by many foreigners in Japan – how vulnerable and helpless they are if they do not belong to some official organization, diplomatic or commercial or cultural or educational. It shows aspects of the often comical predicaments in which less-favoured foreigners like the back-packers and English conversation teachers find themselves trapped. And heaven help you if you are *not* blond and blue-eyed, or if you come from South-East Asia. Racial discrimination poisons Japan.

I have allowed myself a certain amount of satirical observation, but basically it is all true to life as I have known it, off and on, for over thirty years in Japan's great cities, which alas are all now almost exactly alike, all Americanized, all standardized to a stupefyingly boring extent. Most of the Japanese, brain-washed by outmoded conventions, are also peculiarly boring. Fortunately, there are brilliant exceptions, of the kind who appear in this novel. Yet they are precisely the kind of Japanese who are frowned upon by society. They become as much 'outsiders' as the *gaijin*, with the important difference that they are always Japanese and can be reintegrated into the conventional, traditional, often archaic way of life they temporarily rejected. No *gaijin* can be 'reintegrated', because no 'outsider' is ever integrated in the first place. Now a few Japanese young people are being so bold as to rebel against stultifying, age-old sexist conventions.

Partly as a result of Christian missionary activity, the Japanese have developed a strong puritanical streak. Sex rears its lovely head only in secret – in love hotels (often patronized by married couples in search of an hour's privacy), in crowded commuter trains, in night-time parks and in the standing room of packed cinemas, sometimes so brightly lit in attempts to control sexual activity that one can hardly see the movie.

Sex cannot be mentioned in school textbooks, which are censored and 'improved' by the Education Ministry. I had the comic-sad experience of having the word 'love-seat' excised from one of my books in which I was comparing British and American vocabularies. 'Love-seat' is a common Americanism (via Irish) for 'sofa', but officious boobies and academics thought it meant a place for illicit sexual activity. The Ministry also severely limits the range of English vocabulary in textbooks, thus further inhibiting English expression in children and students already repressed by years of non-streamed, highly standardized education.

Nevertheless, my novel is full of the joys of living, however perilously, in the Land of the Rising Sun among the 'with-it' members of what I call 'The Rising Yeneration'.

My portraits and settings are written out of deep affection for Japan, though with a somewhat disabused, wry perception of the comic beneath the sordid, the humour beneath the bureaucratic, much in the style of one of my travel books, *Japan behind the Fan*, which was translated into Japanese and met with considerable approval and success. The Japanese are narcissists. They love to be written about, whether sympathetically or not, especially when the writer is a foreigner. Natives, like Shusaku Endo, express unconventional ideas at their peril.

Yet the foreigner remains that outsider. We can often see him (or her), blond and blue-eyed, chattering away in ephemeral slang clichés like a well-trained pet on TV commercials and quiz shows. Such people bear unlikely names of American origin like Kent or Brad or Melody or Beverly, names that are eagerly appropriated by young people anxious to be 'international' – at the expense of an ugly abbreviation of their often beautiful, noble, native names. They seem so at ease, so at home, these foreign performing apes. But that is only because they have abandoned their foreign identities to conform to the stereotype of the 'outsider' which the Japanese accept most willingly. They have surrendered!

From time to time I feel I cannot stand another minute of life in Japan, can no longer bear being a 'person from outside' who cannot allow himself to become an acceptable cartoon stereotype of the 'mad foreigner'. It is then that the ghastly mutilations of English speech and writing produced by over-reliance on an absurd syllabary for foreign words and names inflict their indescribable pain upon a mind and an ear always attuned to the beauty of the English language. For a writer, that is the most agonizing aspect of Japan – the insensitivity of Japanese English, or as I have called it, 'Janglish'. The Japanese are taking over English wholesale, and making it Japanese. Then, with a horrible physical and spiritual wrench, I drag myself away from friends and colleagues, and seek restoration in Europe. Yet as soon as I get away, I long to go back. This novel is about that cultural dilemma, that love-hatred which lends such intensity to existence, and to human relations.

J.K.

 Contents

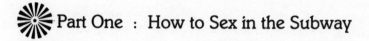# Part One : How to Sex in the Subway

Sex always makes my nose run.
James Kirkup, *Dengonban Messages*: One-line Poems

✻ 1 : April in Sunny Tokyo

✻ 'Why is everyone wearing black?'

It was a carrying voice. Not surprising, perhaps, as its owner, a vivacious blonde, was a regular performer on the provincial stage.

'I do hope I haven't arrived on a day of national mourning!'

Indeed, as they peered out of the low-roofed taxi from the airport, the passers-by did create a drab, though well-dressed, impression. The girls and women were mostly in long, full black skirts and what looked like black orthopaedic shoes with black bobby socks. With their long, lank black hair and droopy, 'deconstructed' black woolly jackets, they looked distinctly trollopish. The men for the most part were no better as they trudged along in almost identical grey or black raincoats. Some younger men, classed as 'students', wore bulky black sweaters or baggy black blousons emblazoned with bold white lettering in incorrect French or English. In addition, there were swarms of schoolchildren, also known as 'students', dressed in all-black uniforms, the girls in old-fashioned, draggy, full-pleated serge gym-dresses and sailor tops, the boys in military-style trousers and jackets with stand-up collars and brass buttons. As nearly everyone had jet-black hair, the general effect was one of Stygian gloom. On the other hand, all the cars and limousines – Toyotas, Hondas, Nissans to a man – were immaculately white, of a blazing squeaky cleanliness that hurt the eyes.

And, in stark contrast to all the rest, there were groups of thuggish-looking young men with close-cropped hair, all dressed in immaculate white double-breasted suits and two-tone highly polished shoes with elevator heels. Naturally, they at once caught Lorelei's eye for a bit of rough trade: 'Who on earth are those heavenly hunks of manhood?'

'*Yakuza*,' replied Hilary, looking them over with equal relish. 'Young mobsters, part-time hooligans belonging to a certain very powerful gang, with influential political connections, particularly in the right-wing nationalist camp.'

'They certainly seem to take a pride in their appearance.'

'And underneath those snow-white garments there are often veritable art treasures . . .'

'What an original way to describe private parts!'

'I mean tattoos, covering most of the body. Real works of Japanese folk-art. Those entering the gangs at the bottom of the ladder prove their sincerity by starting to cover their backs and shoulders with tattoos of leaping carp, flowers, goddesses, legendary heroes . . .'

'How entrancing! I'd love to meet them.'

'You probably will. . . . They like blondes with violet-blue eyes.'

Some of the younger 'students', in drab sports clothes, had the bottoms of their trousers rolled up, though not very far. They looked very unstudious.

'I grow old, I grow old, I shall wear the bottoms of my trousers rolled,' intoned her companion, Major Sitfast, casting an appreciative eye over the occasional neat, boyish rump. The voice was a man's, though one would never have thought it by the sound, which might have been described as 'expensive scent'.

'But why? Why?' Lorelei Thrillingly loved dramatic repetitions. 'Have their mothers and fathers all suddenly died? Or has there been some cataclysmic natural disaster we haven't heard about in the West?'

'Quite possibly, though if there really has been some such calamity, I have failed to notice it. Here in the Land of the Rising Sun catastrophes are a regular feature of daily life and, the longer you live here, the less attention you pay to them. The Japanese for the most part lead lives of such tedious uniformity, they relish every little *shokku* and *boomu*.'

'But hasn't anyone ever told them that black doesn't suit them? They look like funeral candles in a Dracula movie.'

'They're all celebrants of Yoji Yamamoto's black mass.'

But Lorelei had obviously not seen Wim Wender's slavish paean to Yamamoto and his soot-clad handmaidens who would stand in reverent groups around him, ready to hand him a pin or a bit of torn black rag while the Master operated on some helpless model. His girls were given pain-killing drugs before fittings, because of Y.Y.'s notoriously haphazard way with scissors, needle and tacking thread. One devotee who had had a length of black bombazine stapled to her pelvic girdle refused to have it removed and was the envy of all the girls. All Yamamoto fittings had the high drama of TV hospital soap operas – all hands and eyes.

'But those pert little schoolgirls in pleated gym-dresses and middy blouses with sailor collars – they look positively Edwardian!'

She drawled out never-endingly the 'ar' in Edwardian, a trick she had copied from the Queen Mother, whose gracious deportment she much admired, greatly preferring it to the duck-toed waddle of the Queen and the 'my corns are killing me' hobble of Thatcher the Job-Snatcher.

'They're known as "sailors" too,' said Hilary, flapping a hand that looked less than fresh and suddenly screaming 'Hello, sailor!' at no one in particular. 'And in some kinky night-clubs, the hostesses dress in sailor collars and hot pants – which do not flatter most Japanese legs. They appeal to a Japanese male preference for obedient little girls.'

'Are they deliberately trying to create gloom and despondency among the alien population? "Black is for mourning, mourning, mourning – black is for moooourning – and black will do."' She quoted soulfully from a little-known but enchanting Hardy poem she used to be paid to recite at funerals. She had learnt to say 'moooourning' à la Donald Wolfit.

'No, dear, it's just a belated European fashion. You remember how simply everyone a few seasons ago was togged out in various shades of funereal black and clerical grey.'

'But darling Hilary, that was aeons ago!'

'At least five seasons. But even in these days of rapid cultural communication between First World nations, things here always tend to be behindhand.' He was studying the taxi-

driver's plump nape and shaking jowls: he looked not a bit like
the official photo (much younger, and touched up at that) in
the driver's registration tacked above the front window. 'And
besides,' he went on, 'they're quick at picking up new things,
but take for ever to let the old ones go.' He sighed to himself
as he pondered the taxi-driver's lost youth, and his own. He
was on the wrong side of sixty, but despite his carefully dyed
hair, one would never have guessed it. His face was peculiarly
unlined, his eyes bright blue.

'It reminds me of *The Seagull*. Darling Chekhov,' said
Lorelei. 'Nina was one of my best parts at the Ruislip
Rep.'

'Ah, yes, those wonderful opening lines . . .'

'Masha and Medvienko, returning from a walk, enter from
the left.'

'Medvienko. Why do you always wear black?'

'Masha. I'm in mourning for my life. . . .'

Major Sitfast fetched a contented sigh. He, at any rate,
was not in mourning for anything, or anyone, except perhaps
himself.

'And then, after a pregnant pause, she goes on to say: I
am unhappy. Translators, trying to make Chekhov's Russian
sound like suburban English, always translate it as "I'm
unhappy", thus losing the subtle force of the dumbly despairing
"I . . . am . . . unhappy."'

'You do it so beautifully, Lorelei. You sound like
Mrs Siddons calling for a pint of porter.'

'Monster! Tease! Ingrate!'

But even these mock-melodramatic words emerged from
Lorelei's pouted lips, stained a fashionable blueberry-black,
with a ravishingly kittenish purr.

The taxi-driver suddenly said something in Japanese. Hilary
replied, wearily, with a few words in a forbiddingly British
accent.

'What does he want?'

'Nothing. They always ask the same questions: "Where you
from?" Then: "How long stay Japan?" A variation is: "You like
Japan?" It's so predictable it gets boring.'

'I had no idea you spoke Japanese! How clever of you!'

'I don't. Just a few standard responses. Enough to make most Japanese think you must speak the language perfectly. Sometimes I'm afraid just to say "Mitsukoshi", in case the taxi-driver assumes I can speak fluent Japanese, just because I got that simple name right. They all think it's impossible for foreigners to pronounce words of more than one syllable.'

'How sweet.'

'So many men hope to simplify things for you by asking you to call them Brad or Bob or Bud.'

'How awful! But I just love all those Japanese words and names – sushi, Mitsubishi, Takashimaya, shabu-shabu. All so splashy!'

Lorelei Thrillingly had only just arrived for the first time on the shores of Japan. But her words gained the eager approval of the taxi-driver. With a beaming smile, he turned to her and said: 'You have good Japanese speaking', then dissolved into helpless giggles at his own temerity in using English.

'I can see what you mean, Hilary. Speaking the language could become a real nuisance.'

'Fortunately, it's not necessary to learn it,' replied the Major. 'The less you know, the better your students will be pleased. They like full value for their money. They don't want their foreign teachers to teach them in Japanese. Though some do. Mistakenly, in my opinion.'

'What a hideous place!' Lorelei commented.

Their busy highway was lined with ugly, temporary-looking buildings, blocks of dreary apartments, featureless skyscrapers, small, dingy factories, scrap-yards, junk-heaps, occasional small wooden houses seemingly crushed by the weight of concrete around them, and gigantic schools where children were cleaning the windows and sweeping the vast, dusty playgrounds. And everywhere there were unsightly utility poles with dangling wires. Crude neon and painted advertisements filled every spare inch of wall space. It was a vision of Gustave Doré hell. All in primary neon colours, crudely animated.

'The natives don't notice it,' said the Major. 'They are famous for cultivating an eye for beauty. But they have no

sense of ugliness. They just refuse to see anything unpleasant.
Which is a bit of an advantage at times, for outsiders like me.
You can get away with murder, almost.'
    'It's quite a shock for new arrivals.'
    'And you never get used to it. The ugliness is often so
unnecessary, so thoughtless. Like the noise. Amplified voices
everywhere. And the voices of the Japanese are far from
musical, even without microphones.'
    Lorelei was already looking around her with the peculiarly
blank, unseeing boredom of a native. She and Major Sitfast
were riding in an immaculate Toyota taxi. The seats were
spread with freshly laundered white linen covers, neatly fitted
and sedately frilled. There were dinky lace curtains over
the rear windows. A miniature TV set was available for a
small sum. They might almost have been in some suburban
parlour, for there was a small flower arrangement above the
dashboard, though the flowers were, alas, plastic 'Hong Kong
flowers'. The pair had left Tokyo International Airport at
Narita one hour ago, on a wide, modern expressway clogged
with traffic. It was hardly an encouraging introduction to
Japanese life.
    'It usually takes hours and hours to reach the centre,' sighed
Hilary. 'Major' Sitfast was a courtesy title he had bestowed
upon himself. Since arriving in Japan a few years ago, he had
found it an easy way to gain favour with the impressionable
Japanese. As for the British, they did not count. Nor did the
ubiquitous Americans, however much they might think they
did. In Japan, it is the Japanese who really matter. But not
many foreigners realize that. The Major was in that respect a
cut above his colonialist compatriots.
    'That modest, retiring, shrinking-violet pose is all an act,'
Hilary informed Lorelei. 'Under that refined, polite exterior
is a heart of stone. Those butterfly handshakes conceal a fist
of steel.'
    He had appointed himself the director of one of the thou-
sands of small but profitable English Conversation schools that
flourish everywhere in Japan, where the ability to stumble over
a few conventional phrases in an approximate American or
British accent has always been considered the height of chic.

In fact, he was the only teacher in his school, sometimes dignified in the small ads columns of the local English press with the name of 'College' or 'Academy'. Many such fly-by-night educational establishments would add the name 'Cambridge' or 'Oxford' to their names, such false prestige justifying an increase in fees.

The Major's unexpected success in the teaching business had led him to contact Lorelei, a distant cousin, who had often expressed a desire to visit Japan. To an old hand like Hilary, this had seemed a quite inexplicable ambition. But as he now needed an extra teacher, and knowing only too well the low standards of most foreign instructors in Japan, he decided to engage someone he knew had a decent accent and a fairly wide culture – Lorelei Thrillingly. Being a relative, she came cheap. She had a small private income and no ties. At twenty-seven she was still good-looking, in a goofy, blonde bombshell way. She was willing to pay her own air-fare. The Major snapped her up. She would, he knew, be a sensation, with her luxuriant blonde tresses and deep-blue eyes. Just how much of a sensation he could hardly have guessed.

✳ 2 : Japanese Is a Very Splashy Language

✳ I'll give her a year, the Major had thought. That's how long her return plane ticket lasts, anyhow. Then we'll see.

Despite his vague manner, he was quite a good businessman, though in such an unconventional way he hardly knew how he made a living. His needs were modest: he did not smoke, drank only a glass or two of wine, did not run a car – an encumbrance, and an expensive one in Japan – and had no family ties. His only vice, if such it could be called, was a fondness for young men. Japanese youths, once one had divested them of their ugly uniforms, baggy suits and eyeglasses, often revealed enticing bodies, filled with an unexpected passion. Most of them were still 'virgins' as far as women went. But experiences in school Rugby or judo groups, or as demented cheer-leaders, had soon awakened them to 'same-sex love' with their schoolfellows. An affair with a foreigner, and the little extra pocket-money it brought in, was very fashionable. And the Japanese, outwardly prudes, could hardly care less about how their young men seek sexual satisfaction. Incestuous relations with sisters, brothers and even mothers were fairly common: they saw nothing wrong in these things, so they were not wrong. Schoolteachers in particular were considered easy game by youths wanting to pass examinations. So Hilary, as both teacher and head of his academy, was in a strong position. He was able to choose the cream of the males in his classes. One or two, in fact, had received free tuition (and a diploma) for favours granted to the Major, who always treated his lovers well. They were his only weakness, and he did not see why he should not indulge it, to the benefit of both sides.

As the taxi cruised slowly through the streets of central Tokyo on the way to the Vanity Fair Hotel, the Major gazed out of the tinted windows with a jaundiced eye. So many attractive youths – if only one could get one's hands on them! But it was becoming more and more difficult to do so. Was it because he was growing older? (But the young in Japan revere the old, don't they? Perhaps the old don't want to be just revered.) Or was it because increased affluence was making foreigners a less attractive proposition? (Some of his students seemed to be better off than he.) The Major frowned. 'Look at that! You wouldn't have seen anything like that five years ago!'

Lorelei cast bewildered eyes out of the window, attracting the stares of several passing men and not a few women. But she was used to that.

'Those two young ones holding hands – in the street! At one time it was only GIs from Vietnam on R. & R. who did that when they went out with bar hostesses.'

'Well, holding hands in public isn't so very awful, is it?'

'They look like elephants toddling trunk to tail. And it's getting worse. Look at that pair, walking with arms round each other's waists! They even' – he shuddered – 'embrace in public, on the streets, in the subway.' His voice died away on a despairing note: 'It's just not considered proper in traditional society here. Everything's copied from America now. That's one of the reasons Yukio Mishima committed his ridiculous – and so unaesthetic – hara-kiri. He couldn't bear to see Japanese youths getting girls so easily. It's the fault of the girls, really. They've become much too free and easy. Women once knew their place in Japan – in the home, cooking and bringing up kids. Not now. Look at those gaggles of giggling housewives. They descend on the department stores *en masse*, in glutinous gangs. And all the bars now are filled with teenage girls getting drunk. It's abominable.'

'Poor Hilary! It must sometimes be torture for you.'

'The rack! The absolute rack!'

'Never mind. As soon as I get settled, I'll bring you some nice boys.'

'I don't want "nice boys." I can get them easily enough. What I want is just ordinary men – workmen, salarymen, not nancy boys.'

'I'll have to see what I can do.'

They had arrived at the Vanity Fair. The Major paid the driver, who beamed at Lorelei and uttered something that sounded like gargling.

'What did he say?' asked Lorelei.

'Marilyn Monroe.'

'How sweet.'

'They find the pronunciation of "l" and "r" a bit confusing. I hate to think what they'll make of "Lorelei Thrillingly." And they're bad at pronouncing "s" – especially the initial "s" in foreign words and names . . .'

'Oh, Major Sitfast!'

'Yes, indeed. It comes out as "sh. . . ." As you said, Japanese is a very splashy language.'

The taxi door opened automatically. In order to heave himself out of the low door, the Major grasped a semicircular plastic handle hanging on a chain from the seat in front of him.

'It's labelled *sheet holder*,' remarked Lorelei.

'Meaning "seat-holder". You see what I mean about the initial "s"?'

'How shimply shickening.'

The hotel room was small, but comfortable and clean. In the minuscule bathroom a self-adhesive label on the wall gave instructions on how to use the toilet. Stick figures were displayed standing at the 'seat raised' position, and sitting in the 'seat lowered' pose, like Rodin's *Thinker*. Another notice beside the bed warned *No Smoke in Bed! Never Do!*

'Well, that's all clear enough,' Lorelei declared.

'You're here for two nights only,' said the Major, 'to give you time to recover a bit from your jet-lag. Then we'll find you an apartment. I'll meet you in the coffee shop in one hour's time.'

Lorelei prepared her gorgeous body for a lengthy bath. Then she would make a studied toilet. . . . Some of these Japanese men looked like dream-boats.

❋ 3 : The Cynosure of Local Eyes

❋ The coffee shop was packed, mostly with young Japanese couples dawdling the time away over a single cup of coffee. The little waitresses, in white aprons and bobby socks, hardly more than school-leaving age (about sixteen at the most), kept replenishing the water glasses, a not-too-subtle hint that was rarely taken. 'The bottomless cup' had bottomed out.

'They can be really thick-skinned when they want to be,' commented the Major, observing this customer-service ploy.

'Who's "they"?' Lorelei asked. She had changed into a tangerine, pearl-beaded sweater that paid discreet homage to her very shapely breasts. Some Japanese men, and all the women, stared at those breasts as if they could hardly believe their eyes. Most women in Japan seemed to be rather flat-chested, almost boyish in outline. The Major's word for them was 'Japandrogynous'. It applied to many of the boys, too, some of whom had no trouble in passing for female when dressing up in women's garments.

'My dear,' explained the Major, 'you won't be long in Japan before you start referring to the Japanese as "they" and "them". You'll soon find it is a "we" and "they" relationship between the natives and the foreigners, who are not just foreigners but "aliens", as if we came from another planet. The Japanese word for us is *gaijin* – and please don't pronounce it "gay jeans" – which really means, so I've been informed, "a person from outside". We are the outsiders looking in. They are the insiders, also looking in. They're very self-centred. All this talk about internationalism is a load of rubbish, really.'

They had ordered a perfectly Americanized meal of hamburger, coleslaw salad with one eighteenth of a tomato, and coffee. The coffee was terribly thick and strong. Let us leave them to their dinner for a few moments.

Lorelei Thrillingly (not her real name) was a one-time starlet who had never been starleted in anything beyond a few seductive TV commercials. But she had had considerable acting experience, mainly in minor provincial reps, and even, when she was hard up (which was often), taking leads in semi-amateur productions. It always got her a little publicity in the local press and on regional TV.

After having run through the entire gamut of her profession – opening stores, appearing on *What's My Line?* and *This Was Your Wife*, doing a modern-dress *Peter Pan* in astronaut's costume, co-starring with Rock Bottom and the comedy dog star Stupid in a musical about an open prison based on a child's digest version of the Marquis de Sade's *Justine* – she had been told by her agent that the only peak left for her to conquer, at the advanced age of twenty-seven, was a foreign 'art' film. It would mean, of course, appearing in the nude and performing unnatural sex acts. But Lorelei, who had once done, in desperation, a brief stint in a Soho strip club, before being dismissed for incompetence (in her 'Dance of the Seven Veils' she had somehow managed to divest herself of eight), would not mind that kind of 'exposure'.

The agent had dreamt up this weird costume film on a medieval SF theme, to be made in, of all places, Japan. The money was peanuts. But Lorelei had always wanted to experience the inscrutable East which, she felt, must be as 'extreme' as herself. The movie was to be directed by an up-and-coming director who had made his name – Nobuyuki Matsutaka ('Just call me Nob') – in sadistic/voyeurist videos for private closed-circuit transmission in depraved 'love hotels' – houses of assignment, that is, with rooms rented by the hour for the short-time trade, or by the night for bona fide parents seeking a little privacy outside their miniature apartments.

Her co-star was to have been Tadanori Hashimoto ('Just call me Tad, or Hash'), a one-time minor gangster ('discovered' for teenage *yakuza* movies) and homoerotic leader of a bisexual band of teenage hooligans in the Tokyo 'gay quarters' of Asakusa, but now a decidedly untalented pop singer, the idol of all the youth of Japan, which is, practically, all Japan. But he had been caught in bed with a pretty fourteen-year-old schoolboy, sharing a joint. Japan's merciless anti-drug laws induce such self-righteous horror in those who abstain, that poor Hash's career was ruined by the ensuing scandal and the movie project had to be dropped.

But Lorelei had set her mind on seeing Japan: and when it came to something she really wanted to do, there was no holding Lorelei's mind. So here she was, prepared to start at the bottom again, in an English Conversation school, and work her way up, if not to the top, then towards it.

'What's this?' she asked, peering with lovable short-sightedness at a tiny bowl half full of some dim-looking yellow fluid.

'Service. It comes with the hamburger. It's called "corn potage".'

Lorelei took a tentative sip. 'Tastes like face powder flavoured with custard.'

'Yes. Even Western-style food has this rather insipid taste. They even put sugar in the scrambled eggs. They like it that way. Bland. Nothing too flavourful. But they're beginning to develop a taste for real strong curry. It's considered manly.'

The Major sighed over his untasted soup, his rose-tinted monocle on its lavender-velvet cord flashing dispiritedly in the direction of a blue-jeaned 'student' with a copious cow-lick of rich black hair and a remarkable resemblance to L'il Abner. 'Bliss, utter bliss,' he breathed. 'If only I could get my hands on those dusty denim buns.'

As they ate, people kept walking past their table, ostensibly to admire the way they handled knives and forks, but actually to take a sidelong glance from long-slitted, upturned eyes at Lorelei and Hilary. It was no wonder. She had eyes like drenched violets, mouth like a pale carnation, hair a golden copper, and an eager bust that seemed to point in all directions at once, as if mutely clamouring for everyone's undivided attention. As for the Major, it was his pink-tinted monocle that intrigued them. They had never seen anything like it before. How did he keep it screwed in?

Now they had reached the dessert – an apple pie *à la mode* which appeared to consist of soggy cardboard, cheap apple sauce and a stony little hemisphere of vanilla ice. Hilary beckoned for a second cup of coffee. The place had just adopted the American custom of 'the bottomless cup', and the little waitresses did not let you forget it.

'If only the coffee tasted better.'

'I believe it is possible to obtain a type called "American-style". But that's very weak and milky.'

Lorelei finished her pie with a discreet burp of satisfaction, which she prettily disguised as a giggle. Then she turned serious. 'Mmmm,' she growled, in her best imitation of Marlon Brando, a star on whose affectations she modelled her own, with devastating charm. 'Tell me more, Hilary dear. What about the men?'

Already the overnourished ex-starlet was famous for her amours, not always with members of her own sex.

'I feel I can speak with authority on that point,' the Major chaffed. 'They're dream-boats, most of them, just dream-boats. Those lovely sleepy eyes, so bedroomy, those gay smiles – and I really mean gay. Those wonderful lips, those hands, those thighs, those . . .'

'Come to the point, Major,' snapped Lorelei, lighting a gold-tipped cigarette of Balkan extraction. 'How about *that* department?' She crossed her eyes in a meaningful way.

'Well,' the Major sighed regretfully, 'many of them *are* on the small side, but usually quite perfectly formed, you know. Personally I used to prefer the rather stocky kind. And of course there are some fine-built, well-set-up ones, too. College football or rugger players, for example, always good for at least *one* press photo, dear, and always *dying* to practise their very limited English. It's always the weedy, bespectacled ones who speak the best English. The good-looking ones don't need to. Then there are those enormously fat sumo wrestlers, terribly good-natured. And the occasional priest or student monk can be most exciting.'

'Maybe I'd like a small one, for a change,' breathed Lorelei in a tone of fond reminiscence, as if reviewing, in her mind's eye, the various engorged members of a whole battalion of troopers. Speculative sharpness glittered like crushed ice in her dew-drenched eyes, whose deep violet blue, in moments of passion, sometimes took on the intensity of black pansies.

Though not exactly a nymphomaniac, she liked to have at least one man – preferably a different one – each day. Already she had begun to suspect she had had her fill of grinning, muscle-bound ape-men, who were usually all muscle and very little else. Big but useless. If she had to squeeze one more sunburnt bicep at a village fête, she would, she felt, scream. Women she loved. But she absolutely refused to masturbate – it seemed so self-indulgent, almost immoral.

They shimmered out of the coffee shop. She looked intriguing, and she knew it, with her dripping, diamond-type earring lustres which she wore even at breakfast. Her long, lissom legs were slinky in pure silk stockings, sheer heaven to wear with a mink suspender belt, and with those unusual seams running up the backs of her shapely calves, knee-pits and limpid thighs. She was certainly the cynosure of local eyes, as she hobbled, with fake helplessness, on extravagantly sharp high heels. The Major swayed, too, not to be outdone, in the manner of an elderly cowboy wearing a hobble skirt. On Lorelei's rather plump hands were numerous large 'stage' rings which she had stolen from the Old Vic during a brief appearance there as a delinquent Desdemona, playing opposite a celebrated black American trumpeter as Othello. He had been 'hailed by the critics' because whenever he got bored with the play – which was often – he would pick up his horn and blow some spine-chilling blues, much to the delight of the equally bored audience. Her own performance had gone practically unnoticed, even though in her final scenes she had worn nothing at all under her Baby Doll nightie, and had hidden the hanky provocatively in a most unexpected place.

The Major saw Lorelei to the elevator. 'I'll leave you here,' he told her, his eyes attracted by a passing bus-boy's bum. 'Have a good night, and I'll call for you in the morning around eleven-thirty.'

Lorelei gave her famous yawning smile.

'Then we'll have lunch, and go and see the sights. There's even a Disneyland, just out of town.'

She groaned. 'You can keep it.'

The elevator arrived and they pecked at each other, taking care not to disturb their make-up. 'You may kiss me, but don't be rough,' giggled Hilary. 'Now what Somerset Maugham play did that come from?'

'Search me.'

'He's very popular in Japan. The students call him "Sunset Mum".'

'How appropriate.'

The Major darted away after his unsuspecting prey, his rose-tinted monocle dancing ahead of him on the end of its levender cord like a fairy spirit.

As the elevator oozed its way up to the twentieth floor of the Vanity Fair, Lorelei listened to one of the latest hit tunes coming from the Muzak that sometimes seems to be bandaging the whole of Japan in very sticky musical wallpaper:

> If you want coffee,
> Go to Brazil,
> And go to Spain
> For the matador's kill,
> But if you want a man –
> Go to Japan.
> You can't fail –
> It's the Tokyo Tale.

✺ 4 : Caresses and Coffee

✺Lorelei had no intention of getting up before noon the next day. She usually regarded three in the afternoon as a civilized hour to rise from sheets the shade of a wood-nymph's thigh. And she never went to bed before four in the morning.

But tonight was different. It was only eleven, but she felt sleep stealing over her body like the hands of several lovers in a gang-bang orgy of the greatest refinement. A *partouze* in paradise was how she described slumber.

Before sinking into the arms of Morpheus, however, she sat up in bed under the queen-size quilt and watched some late-night TV. It was mostly weather reports: at first she thought it was urgent news of an advancing army, as the maps of the islands of southern and western Japan became suffused with a pretty rose. But apparently they were intended to show the gradual progress of opening, and falling, cherry blossom on its pink-and-white-petalled path to the remote north, where snow still lay on the mountains.

Then there were seemingly interminable news reports about the latest doings in Parliament, which she discovered was called the Diet. The faces of all those middle-aged and elderly politicians gave her the shudders. How on earth could people bring themselves to vote for men with such plain and downright ugly visages? Some of them looked like crooks who had made crime pay. Others were like degenerate dwarfs or effete fools. The Minister for Defence was a pop-eyed schoolboy swot behind owlish eyeglasses. One or two resembled Ancient Romans – the sort who conspired to slaughter Julius Caesar. There was one old gentleman, obviously a top banana, who reminded her of the short-sighted Mr Magoo of the popular animated cartoons of her childhood. How they all droned on! Did anyone ever watch this stuff?

She switched channels and was rewarded by the sight of a semi-nude model perched on a high stool, hands clasped round one drawn-up knee, and simpering with a touching innocence as she ogled the camera crew. She was badly in need of a dentist's attentions, for she had the most awful snaggle-teeth, which gave her a slightly vampirish look. As everyone knows, in the West snaggle-teeth are regarded as the attributes of a witch, but Lorelei was to discover that they are considered 'charm points' in the young ladies of Japan. The sight made her shudder slightly, and she crossed herself with practised fluency – she had once gone on a summer school training course for incipient nuns, but had been expelled for 'bawdy behaviour and blasphemy'.

Well, thought Lorelei, as the 'TV talent' squirmed with would-be seductiveness on her high stool, I could do better than that. . . .

With this enticing possibility of lucrative employment in mind, she fell into a fitful doze, in which she dreamt of being hijacked by attentive terrorists.

But jet-lag had caught up with her, and she found herself wide awake at six in the morning. She had forgotten to switch off the television set, and now found herself staring at a picture of the Rising Sun flag – a bold crimson disc on a pure white ground – blowing in a high wind on the screen. Grave, mysterious music was being played. The national anthem perhaps? Then a bilious-looking announcer started reading the news, which was just a repetition of the previous evening's. Then there was another long weather report, with lots of maps, and a tiny Mount Fuji symbol, in blue, with a bit of snow on the idealized peak.

Lorelei felt wide awake. It was no use trying to go back to sleep. To her horror, she found that breakfast would not be served until seven-thirty, and there was no room service. The mini-fridge contained bottles of Sapporo beer, fizzy drinks, sake and small vials of a revolting 'stamina beverage'. But there was a thermos flask of boiling water, and there were some tea-bags containing green tea. She made a cup, lifting it in both hands, as there was no handle on the cup. It had a curious, bitter but refreshing taste, and the delicate green colour was delightful in the white china with the blue designs.

She drew the curtains and looked down into the street. Already there were lots of people hurrying to work, nearly all of them bareheaded, dressed in black, dark grey or dawn fawn coats. The men all wore suits with white shirts and conservatively striped ties. They looked grim. Lorelei again got the impression that she had arrived for some dead statesman's funeral. Traffic was beginning to pile up at the crossings, where the pedestrians stood dutifully waiting for the lights to turn green before crossing the road. Even when there was no traffic coming, they waited patiently for the green light. Then they would scurry across the black-and-white-striped crossing – the mass mind in consensual motion.

Amid all this grimness Lorelei glimpsed in the distance some touches of pink. What could it be? Ah yes, cherry blossom, great domes of it in some small public park. At that hour it was almost the only touch of colour in the capital, apart from the few neon signs on neighbouring impassive blocks of concrete and glass. The red-and-green traffic signals added jewel-like points in the general drabness.

By the time she had showered, dressed and put on some make-up, it was only seven o'clock, so Lorelei decided to take a stroll in the streets while waiting for the coffee shop to open for breakfast. She rode down to the lobby in an empty elevator. This time the Muzak was some kind of twanging instrument like an untuned harp. The lobby was empty. A clerk at the reception desk bowed as she handed him her room key. She gave him a smile, but he did not respond. His face was thin and sallow, the eyes narrow and cold. But Lorelei knew men too well to be taken in by this unwelcoming attitude. She was fully aware that behind her back he was mentally undressing her as she tastefully tottered on her six-inch heels to the revolving door, which she allowed almost to embrace her as it slowly, seductively revolved.

The April morning was fresh but humid under the early sun. There was a sort of feverish dazzle in the air. Lorelei had put on an open-work peach silk blouse with a pair of very moulding jade-green tights. From a certain distance, she looked topless:

the sleeveless blouse was almost exactly the same colour as her peachy skin. She really stood out in that subdued and rather gloomy workaday crowd. She walked with a smile on her lovely, chiselled lips, as if she did not have a care in the world. Busy as everyone seemed to be, she attracted many glances – of admiration, of course, but also of puzzlement. At that time of day, no other woman in the streets was dressed as she was. The passing buses were packed: men straphanging in them bent down to watch her as the buses eased through the traffic. Groups of small children, all wearing identical uniforms, stared at her in astonishment. Older schoolchildren started to giggle, the girls holding hands across their mouths in a way that Lorelei found impolite. To titter behind a raised hand was 'not done' in educated English circles, especially when the object of the hilarity was a human being. She began to feel slightly irritated. One of the bigger girls, greatly daring, called out to her: 'Harrow!' 'No, dear, Cheltenham Ladies' College,' Lorelei replied with a sweet, good-natured smile. The girl looked at her in puzzlement, then broke into fresh giggles and took to her heels with her two bosom friends, their long gym-dresses flapping round bandy legs. On their feet were sturdy black shoes and pastel bobby socks. Others were wearing scuffed sneakers. Most of the schoolboys, too, were in sneakers or running shoes of the latest design, but invariably grubby. It spoilt the smart effect of the uniforms – at least of those that were pressed and clean.

Lorelei had intended just to stroll round the block. But the press of people was now so great that she decided to turn back to the hotel. In a crowd at a crossing, waiting for the lights to change, she had distinctly felt someone's hands on her rump – a rather dubious compliment. When she turned round to give her attacker a piece of her mind, she found herself looking into the mild, plain face of a middle-aged, bespectacled businessman. His expression was completely blank. Could it have been he? Unsure of herself, Lorelei gave him the benefit of the doubt. She felt rather relieved to be back in her hotel, despite the guarded look of the desk clerk as he handed her the key.

By now breakfast was being served. She entered the coffee shop and took a seat at a small table beside the window, which looked out upon a miniature dry stone garden with a small waterfall and a clump of dusty bamboos round an unstable-looking stone lantern. There were only one or two other people in the coffee shop. The Muzak was 'Land of Hope and Glory' sung in Japanese by what sounded like a massed choir of castrati.

The little bobby-socked waitress handed her a bilingual menu, from which Lorelei chose the 'American Breakfast' – coffee, orange juice, scrambled eggs with processed ham, toast and jam. There was only one tiny cup of coffee in the doll's tea-set pot, and only one slice of toast – but it was very thick, the kind that in England is described as a 'doorstep'. The Major was right: the scrambled eggs had been sweetened, and tasted terribly insipid. Lorelei heaved a sigh. She always needed at least three cups of coffee to start her day. So, signalling to the waitress, she flashed her a brilliant smile and said: 'May I have another pot?' The little waitress bent double, as if pole-axed, and seemed helpless with mirth as she ran away to fetch a young man with a wildly pretty face and spiky bangs who appeared to be the maître d'hôtel. Bowing and smiling at her with rather too perfect teeth, he said: 'Please again, very slow please.' Not taking any chances this time, Lorelei indicated her coffee cup, and breathed: 'More coffee?' The youth instantly understood, answered 'Hai-hai' (which, Lorelei knew, means 'Yes') and dashed off to the kitchen. After a moment the little waitress, having regained her composure, came positively running with a pot of coffee on a tray and, with a gentle, shy smile, poured a fresh cup for Lorelei, who felt she was beginning to get the hang of things.

As she was leaving, the young waiter bowed to her at the desk and murmured 'Very foolish girl', which for a moment Lorelei thought to refer to herself. However, he merely meant the little waitress, who was standing right next to him, again overcome by giggles. She was apparently accustomed to being referred to in this manner in English.

When Lorelei reached her room, she found that an English-language newspaper, *The Nippon News*, had been shoved under her door, 'With the Compliment of the Manager'.

She lay down on the unmade bed and idly leafed through it. She was one of those sensible people who never open a newspaper, finding them mentally constipating and spiritually degrading. Besides, they soil one's hands, unless (as the Major did) one wears a light pair of white silk gloves when holding the filthy pages. But Lorelei had nothing better to do before refreshing her make-up, and she felt a faint curiosity about what was going on in Japan. However, she was deeply disappointed to find that the 'news' was nearly all American, couched in the American language, and in that hideous, simplified spelling. The bits of news about Japan – the Diet, a coming election, trade imbalances, *yakuza* activities, taxes and medical matters were totally boring, as were the many feature articles on cookery, fashion, gossip, 'embassy row' chatter, inscrutable cartoons, inane letters from readers who seemed to be mental cases and so on.

The most interesting part was the small ads. There were scores of requests for 'native English conversation teachers' – none of them stated what salary would be paid or what the conditions were. There were also some ads for 'bunny girls' and 'tall, blonde foreign hostesses' and 'lovely escorts for salaried workers' at places with odd names like Club Funny (a misprint for Club Fanny? Lorelei wondered) and Holy Hock Heaven. Applicants were desired to send photos ('returnable') of themselves 'in bikinis or shorts'. Lorelei tucked away this information in her memory bank: it might come in useful one day. One never knew. . . .

A small news item on the back page caught her eye: the police were 'cracking down on the 'No-Pan' coffee shops and clubs'. Apparently at these places the waitresses wore no panties, only aprons. There were similar dens of vice employing only young boys. This development cheered Lorelei up considerably. So life was not all flower arrangement and boring old tea ceremony.

✻ 5 : Cherry Blossom Charms

✻ The Major arrived just before noon, thirty minutes late. He had been stuck in a traffic jam and was looking fairly bilious at having to pay so much extra for his taxi.

'It's ghastly, my dear, sitting in that tiny taxi in the rush-hour and watching the yen click up inexorably. Sometimes I just jump out and walk. It's often quicker. But this time the cabbie was rather gorgeous, with those lovely high cheekbones which always turn me on, so I stayed with him right to the end, pretending to be a first-time tourist and squeezing his muscular shoulder from time to time – so good-natured, just up from the country, hardly knew where he was going anyhow. When I finally arrived here we were the best of friends and he handed me a miniature cake of toilet soap – service, he said, though he pronounced it 'sarbus', which was all part of the charm, you know. It has put me in quite a good mood for the day. I cancelled all classes, so we have time to wander round and see some of the sights.'

'Hilary, you are a scream.'

Lorelei had wanted to say 'screamer' but stopped herself just in time. After all, the Major was her future employer.

The Major was wearing, this bright April morn, an almost too well-cut safari suit in an intriguing tone of bitter lemon with a gold belt and buttons – well, gilt anyhow – and a pulsingly violet shirt with a fat, knitted white necktie. His trouser bottoms were tucked into Cuban-heeled, matching violet, high suede boots hung with gilt chains, and he was today wearing a sumptuous gold-rimmed violet monocle with a lemon-yellow ribbon to complete the ensemble.

When Lorelei saw how he was rigged out, she felt distinctly peeved, for she had changed into simple designer jeans, sandals and black leather jacket over a T-shirt she had found in the hotel shop emblazoned with the Janglish slogan *We Live, We Love!*

'Just wait a sec!' She darted into the elevator and went up to her room.

The Major paced the hotel lobby, ogling the boys in their pillbox hats and fawn bum-freezers. He even winked at the dyspeptic-looking desk clerk, who did not react. No skin off *my* nose, Hilary thought with self-satisfied good humour, which dropped a few degrees when he saw Lorelei emerge from the elevator. Not to be outdone by the Major, she had carelessly knotted a scintillating gold and scarlet length of sari material round her exquisite throat, letting it trail and billow behind her as she shimmered towards him. Her unbelievably slim and shapely ankles were adorned with loosely fitting gilt handcuffs, joined by a length of delicate gold chain that allowed her to take only small, mincing steps. And on her pearly ear-lobes, among the dripping chandeliers of brilliants, hung sets of tiny silver bells that chimed merrily every time she moved her fetchingly silly little head.

The Major knew he could not compete with that, so he merely raised his well-manicured hands and wreathed his raddled features in a false smile, saying, with Berlitz fluency, 'Mah!' – which is Japanese for 'My!' But privately he was swiftly pondering how he could prevail upon her to remove those constricting – what could one call them? – 'feetcuffs?' On the other hand, they gave her the helpless look adored by Japanese men. 'I thought we might stroll over to Ueno Park to see the last of the cherry blossom,' he icily suggested. 'We can visit the Toshogu Shrine, then have a Japanese lunch in a neat little restaurant I know. Afterwards, perhaps a visit to the Art Museum. . . ?'

'I'm in your hands, dear boy,' Lorelei gushed at him, pouting in her best Marilyn Monroe manner. 'But what's so special about looking at some old cherry blossom? I always associate it with that make of British boot polish.'

'My dearest,' explained the Major, guiding her along the crowded pavements, a bejewelled hand on her rather bony elbow, 'you must realize that the Japanese are obsessed by cherry blossom. It's the symbol of human life and its passing beauty, its frailty. So they love to sit and sigh sentimentally over the falling petals, at the same time cheering themselves up with enormous flagons of rice wine. Tears fill their eyes if a cherry blossom petal falls in the cup. The more artistic make up little poems called *haiku*, consisting of seventeen well-chosen syllables, something like:

> Even at cherry
> blossom-viewing time, I think
> of this painful world.

'or:

> Among the blossoms
> of the cherry, the sparrows
> drop their shit on you.

'That sort of thing . . . I laiku haiku . . .'
'Really, Major Sitfast!' cried Lorelei in mock-reproof.
'Oh, they sometimes compose worse ones than that.'
'Save them for later, dear, when I can appreciate them in comfort.'

The street was hardly the place for composing or listening to haiku, however robust in tone. Though it was not a public holiday, just an ordinary working morning, the pavements were crowded with businessmen in joyless groups trudging to lunch at some noodle-stall or fast-food cafeteria. It was fairly mild weather, and sunny, so they were mostly in shirt-sleeves, but as they moved along with their peculiarly graceless walk they kept their hands in their trouser pockets, and as some of them were slopping along in cheap sandals they gave the impression of gaggles of amputated hens. Their cheap but crisp white shirt-sleeves and their eyeglasses kept flashing blankly in the sun. Overhead, there were sprays of fluorescent pink plastic cherry blossoms fixed over every shop door, but only Lorelei noticed these charmless manifestations of the season's traditional regret for the passing of youth, because these blossoms could not fall. So they were just meaningless decorations.

Lorelei attracted many curious glances, and not only from men. One young woman in a long, trollopy black frock and a black overcoat down to below her knock knees, stopped Lorelei and said, pointing to her ankles: 'Where you get? I will buy.'

Lorelei looked at the Major, wondering what to say. He replied, with glib fluency: 'Takashimaya. Fourth floor. Yon-kai.'

The young woman uttered breathless thanks – 'Domo arigato gozaymasu' – and immediately hailed a taxi to take her to Takashimaya department store in the Ginza.

'They want to be the first with everything these days,' commented Hilary while his monocled eye strayed over the portly posterior of a particularly samurai-like policeman, who was, however, gaping only at Lorelei. Then, in a sudden joking gesture, he jingled his own pair of real steel handcuffs at her, giving a glad guffaw and a broad grin. Lorelei flounced past him, dimpling.

Bands of students and schoolchildren passed them from time to time, convulsed with giggles, the girls almost collapsing with mirth as they held their big red hands over their wide-open mouths. Many were the cries of 'Harrow!' and *'Gaijin!'*

'That's all they know how to say in English – "Harrow!" – after ten years of classes,' the Major said scornfully. 'Take no notice of them or of the words. They're catcalls, really. But it's good for *my* line of business when Japanese teachers of English are so incompetent. I can teach a boy more English in a week than they can in a year. And now they've reduced the teaching hours of English in schools to two a week, I'm getting more and more private pupils and bigger classes. That's where *you* come in, darling.'

'I can't wait to give my first lesson,' sighed Lorelei. 'Some of these high-school boys look rather choice.'

'If you can only get your hands on them and shuck them out of those hatefully ugly black uniforms, you may find a treasure. The only really exciting thing for me about those high-school uniforms is the divine fragrance of stale adolescent sweat that emanates from the armpits and the crutch. If I had the skills to turn it into a saleable perfume, I'd call it 'Flowers of Lethe', with just a touch of chloroform to overcome any last resistance.'

There were housewives strolling and shopping, some of them in drab kimonos, some of them in even drabber modern dress. The impression of mournful blackness was everywhere. It had a standardizing effect on people's appearance. A group of tough-looking, crop-headed youths in unusually broad-striped suits, cigarettes stuck like thermometers in the corners of their cruel mouths, slouched past them. They gave our pair a practised scowl.

'Young *yakuza*,' whispered Hilary after they had passed. 'Belonging to some gangster organization. Just like big business, really, though they do resort to violent means sometimes, shoot-outs and murders and arson. Some of them are weirdly attractive, tattooed all over with the most grotesque designs. They look marvellous in the public bath or when they're displaying their artistic tattoos, wearing breech-clouts or *fundoshi* – marvellous word, dear, do remember it – showing off whatever they've got, which is often disappointingly little in the way of sexual equipment. But they rather endearingly refer to their balls as *kintama* or 'eggs of gold'. Get that!'

He was nodding his head towards a blue-jeaned delivery boy with a rolled white towel round his shaven pate, and wearing a cheerful blue-and-white cotton happi-coat stamped with the name of the shop he worked for, apparently a food shop or restaurant, because he was cycling gaily through the heavy traffic with only one hand on the handlebars and a pile of lacquer boxes of food on one shoulder. He flashed an amiable smile at the Major and gave him a wink. But then he took in Lorelei and, so great was his astonishment, he fell off his bike in front of a cruising loudspeaker van touting the public for old newspapers and magazines in exchange for a few toilet-rolls. The van pulled up just in time as the bike and the boy skidded among coils of steaming noodles and slices of raw fish. He picked himself up unhurt, collected his boxes and what bowls remained unbroken, jumped on his bike and pedalled off as cheerfully as ever, waving to the Major and Lorelei.

'A treasure,' wailed the Major. 'If only I could have read the name of his restaurant, I'd have taken you there for lunch. Think of being served by angels like that!'

By now they had reached the park and started wandering among the ancient cherry trees, past their best unfortunately. But still there were great domes of white and pale pink blossom overhead, casting down gentle, lingering snowstorms of petals on groups of revellers, mostly working men, who sat drinking sake and eating rice balls under the spreading branches. These working lads were wearing baggy pants nipped tightly round the calves and knees, rather like outsize jodhpurs, and on their feet were split-toed sock-shoes with rubber soles.

'Why, they're very fashionably dressed!' cried Lorelei. 'Those jodhpurs are the latest thing. I wish I'd brought mine – imperial violet!'

'But for them, they are just ordinary working clothes,' the Major informed her. 'All that bagginess round the thighs is supposed to act as a kind of parachute if they should fall while working on a construction site. And, my dear, get those bright chiffon scarves they wear round their manly throats! Camp as all get-out, did they but know it. And, fortunately, they don't.'

Some of the workmen had broken off small sprigs of cherry blossom and stuck them in the rolled white towels they wore on their heads.

'The towels are really a symbol of effort, of hard work, as well as of manly energy. Oh, Lorelei, I think that lot are inviting us to join in their revels!'

A small group of young working apprentices, possibly training to be carpenters, were beckoning to the *gaijin* pair, offering them small cups of rice wine.

'Is it all right?' Lorelei asked anxiously, as the beaming Major made a bee-line for the youths.

'Of course, darling. They look tough, but they're dolls really, quite harmless. And when they've had a bit to drink, they're ever so funny and good-natured.'

The six or seven young workmen were sitting on bits of old tatami on which were spread lunch-boxes, bowls of pickles, some fruit and several bottles of sake. The men cleared a space for the Major and Lorelei, who had to shake hands with each one in turn. The boys, whose work-roughened hands were quite clean, made an exaggerated display of wiping their palms on their backsides before offering their hands. They stood up to do this, bowing, and nearly falling down with laughter at the unusual sensation of shaking hands with foreigners. They had no English, and Hilary had little Japanese, but they all got on famously together, quaffing one cup of sake after another, taking care to invite each other one by one, pouring for each other with ceremonious gaiety.

Then they started singing and clapping their hands, and soon the Major and Lorelei were dancing in a ring with their hilarious hosts, learning the minimal steps and ribald gestures of a northern folk-dance. They soon picked it up, to the great delight of the large crowd that had gathered round to watch and applaud them.

At the end of the performance, they toasted each other in final cups of sake, and with many a soulful *sayonara* they parted, the boys going off to work, and our English visitors to look for some Japanese food. After all the cups of sake, they were feeling very merry. For a long time Lorelei and the Major remembered the healthy faces of those working lads, flushed a delicate dogrose pink by the wine, and their strong, manly singing voices, the butterfly grip of their horny hands.

✳️ 6 : Art for the Masses

✳️ They walked round Shinobazu Pond, its murky, bottle-green surface flecked with white and pink petals, which in places had gathered into snowy drifts of blossom, like foam after a storm. The willow trees hung down weeping, showing the first tender green of leaves which stirred gently in the wind. There were paper lanterns all round the lake. From the nearby zoo came the bellowing of some bored lion.

'This place will do, I think,' said the Major, pausing outside a small restaurant in traditional style. The front was all pale wood, looking fresh and clean, and over the doorway hung a little indigo blue curtain, rather like a divided pelmet, announcing the name of the place in inscrutable white calligraphy. In the window a few tempting dishes of seafood and sushi were displayed. They looked absolutely delicious but were made of plastic. There was also a sober, refined flower arrangement and the figure of a cat with its left paw raised to ear-level, beckoning them in. It was a charming gesture of invitation.

They dipped their heads under the curtain's divided segments, Hilary taking great care not to ruffle his carefully arranged perm. He had had a sort of pale ginger rinse which effectively disguised the strands of silver in his diminishing curls.

As they entered the restaurant, there was an explosive welcoming shout that sounded to Lorelei like 'Scrrrratch my back' but which, the Major informed her, with proud authority, was 'Irrashaimasu' – the traditional greeting for customers. There was a long, plain wooden counter at which they took their places on rather wobbly stools. A girl trotted up to them in a dark cotton kimono and handed them steaming hot towels.

'Just use them on your hands, dear,' Hilary advised Lorelei. 'These hot towels, deliciously perfumed sometimes, come from mass suppliers, and in some establishments I shan't mention at lunch-time they are used by naughty bar hostesses for illicit purposes, which I shall describe in detail later on. Of course they have been washed and sterilized, but all the same it's considered very un-chic to wipe one's face with materials of such doubtful origin. Nevertheless, some men give themselves a proper going-over with such towels, not only face and neck but also, in summertime, forearms when they're wearing short-sleeved summer shirts. I've even seen them, when wearing shorts, wiping their legs with them. Personally, I just dab behind my ears, where one does sometimes develop a certain stagnant area in this humid weather. Don't disturb your simply exquisite make-up, you theatrical thing!' He gave her a playful slap.

Lorelei merely patted her palms with her towel. It was certainly refreshing, as her hands felt somewhat damp and dewy.

'In the torrid heat of midsummer, the towels are chilled. Now that's really a treat. I allow myself to mop my fevered brow.'

The little waitress served them with large, thick mugs of green tea, and laid chopsticks in paper sheaths before them. There were two men behind the counter making sushi and cutting up raw tuna and octopus for sushi or fresh sashimi slices. They started with slices of raw fish, two kinds of tuna, lean and fatty. They were coolly delicious, dipped in soy sauce flavoured with green horse-radish, and slipped down Lorelei's lovely long throat with the utmost ease. The two men making sushi paused for a moment to watch what effect the raw fish had on the *gaijin*, and were delighted when the Major signalled for more. Two small bottles of heated sake were served. Then they had a variety of tasty sushi and finally a lacquer bowl of clear soup with a few button mushrooms and a small leaf in it.

Lorelei was charmed. 'I feel as if I've been waiting all my life to taste this kind of food. It's simply heavenly. I could go on eating it for ever. And I'm sure it must be good for the health.'

'And for the figure, we hope,' added the Major, smoothing the skirts of his safari jacket over matronly hips as they stood up

to go. As they left the restaurant, everyone chorused something
Lorelei heard as 'fatter noses' but which turned out to be *Mata
dozo*, meaning 'Come back again s')n'. And they sounded as if
they really meant it!

'What charming people!' murmured Lorelei.

'Let's go and relax and recover from all that sake,' said
Hilary. 'I feel quite squiffy. Let's go to the Toshogu Shrine
first, to pay our respects to the gods of this infuriating land.
Seventeenth century, love. All these bronze and stone lanterns
make a pretty effect leading up to the holy of holies, don't
they? It's called a 'National Treasure'. I need hardly add
that I prefer other types of national treasures, human ones,
preferably young and male.'

'Shall I ever find my own national treasure here, I wonder?'

'Seek and ye shall find.'

'I certainly intend to.'

'Over there is the famous Ueno belfry, which we are told
often figures in Japanese poetry. You can come and sound
the bell at New Year. And just a little way away you can see
the Seiyoken Restaurant, Western style and quite delightful
in a Victorian sort of way. It also has literary associations,
though I'm not quite sure what. Nearly everything in Japan
has literary associations.'

'How intellectual.'

'Not really. You won't meet many real intellectuals in Japan.
Of course there are a lot of fake ones, as in every country. Wait
until you meet the intellectual cream of our own land, the
British Cultural Society . . . Then you'll see some genuine
fakes.'

They passed several university buildings and various mu-
seums until they came to the National Museum of Western
Art. It was terribly crowded for an exhibition of Renoir
nudes. They could hardly see the pictures for the people.
Fortunately, they were taller than most of the Japanese
visitors, so could view the exhibits over a choppy sea of
black hair.

The Major groaned. 'All these gross female nudes. They look
as if they'd been painted with strawberry jam.'

'Why are they so popular?'

'The Japanese adore female nudes, especially those by Western artists. The annual exhibitions of painting groups at the Tokyo Metropolitan Fine Art Gallery are full of female nudes. The depiction of pubic hair is forbidden by law in Japan . . .'

'How quaint!'

'So the artists have to exercise some ingenuity to convey the impression of hair 'down there' by colouring, shading and so on. When you see pornographic photos taken here, you'll see that the vaginal area has been erased – it's more obscene than the real thing could ever be. It's the same in the movies – The slightest revelation of pubic hair is scratched out by the censor.'

'No wonder so many Japanese men look frustrated.'

'The censors employ an army of unemployed, senior citizens, and even students, to black out the nudes in *Playboy* magazine and other sexy periodicals from overseas. Yet there is a long tradition of erotic art by celebrated artists like Utamaro. It's erotic fantasy, really, because the male sexual parts they depict are so fabulously exaggerated.'

'Presumably to compensate for the smallness of the real thing.'

'Exactly. That's all part of the Japanese inferiority complex. But those magnificent works of erotic art, called *shunga*, are banned. They can never be shown in public, and it's an offence to reproduce them and sell them. So much for Japanese prudery and hypocrisy. They go hand in hand with raging masturbatory fantasies.'

'But these pictures by Renoir cannot be called pornographic or obscene.'

'Not even the censor could airbrush them out. Personally, I find all female nudes disgusting, and a good many male ones too. But you rarely see a male nude in Japan, either in painting or in sculpture. The male figure is not considered aesthetically pleasing. But I get the impression that the Japanese don't want to degrade the male by portraying him naked. Women are inferior beings here, so it doesn't matter if they are shown nude, and the omission of pubic hair is just a token respect paid to the female sex, which after all does include sacred images like mothers and sisters and female deities.'

'Really, Hilary, I had no idea you could be so serious.'

'You'd be surprised. My ambition is to open an art museum in which there would be no female nudes at all, only male studies and still lives.'

'Well, that might keep the number of visitors down to manageable proportions.'

As she spoke, Lorelei felt herself being jostled on all sides by the surging crowds of Renoir enthusiasts. She suddenly felt something hard pressing against her bottom. Putting a hand behind her, she found herself stroking the front of a young man's trousers, in which an erect penis unmistakably pulsed. It was a neatly dressed youth with a mane of rich black hair – an artist, obviously. As her eyes encountered his, he flushed guiltily and walked away, holding his exhibition catalogue over the spreading dark stain the orgasm had left on the front of his trousers. Well, that was a quick one, thought Lorelei. I hope they're not all afflicted with premature ejaculation.

'You lucky girl' was Hilary's comment. He had been observing the young man's actions and had even managed to encourage them by slipping his own hand round Lorelei back, withdrawing only when the youth was obviously reaching a climax. 'No censorship in that department,' he added. 'Wait until you start riding the rush-hour subway and the surface lines. Unlike the Paris Métro, where the favoured carriage for sex play is the second from the front, here in Japan it's always the last, second last or first carriage that attracts the sensation-seekers. Of both sexes. But some women do raise a hue and cry against *chikan* – that is, male molesters. As far as I know, there's no term for men who 'molest' men, or for women molesters, either. I've had many a grope in the crush, thinking it was the handsome young office clerk pressed hard against me, only to find out, too late, that it was some delicate female fingers on my crutch.'

But jet-lag was again catching up with Lorelei. She begged the Major to take her back to the Vanity Fair. They went by subway, to avoid the traffic hold-ups in the streets, but it was not yet the rush-hour, so Lorelei had to be satisfied with a red plush seat just vacated by a sturdy young high-school student who had been admiring her legs. The seat was boiling hot.

Climbing the subway stairs back to the street was something of a trial with her feetcuffs, though the gilt chain was long enough for her to negotiate the steps. She decided that in future she would wear these unusual adornments only on formal occasions, when she was less likely to need to run for her life.

'Now, Lorelei dear, have a good night's rest. Dinner in the coffee shop's quite decent. I'll be calling for you around ten tomorrow morning, so please have your bags packed. We're going to find you an apartment. It may take awhile. Monday I'll introduce you to your first class. I can tell you, they're all agog to meet you. Tomorrow's Saturday, so there are no classes. The weekend should give you time to settle in. See you tomorrow, darling.'

They exchanged cheek-pecks, and Lorelei ankled her dreamy way into the elevator. The Muzak was playing 'Thriller'. How very suitable, Lorelei thought, for one of the Thrillingly family. Alone in the lift, she did a frenzied shimmy as the cage oozed heavenwards.

But one thing was bothering her. In that morning's small ads she had been stunned by the colossal rents demanded for apartments. How can I ever pay one million yen a month for my pad? she wondered. How on earth shall I make ends meet?

❋7 : Shock after Shock

❋Lorelei slept the fitful, nightmarish sleep of the jet-lagged. She kept waking up in the dark and wondering where she was. Before retiring, she had drunk three or four cups of green tea, and these seemed to keep her mind ablaze with imagery, much of it lustful and thick with sexual symbolism. Japan's feeble imitation of the Eiffel Tower, called Tokyo Tower, appeared to her tightly encased in a gigantic, transparent condom dangerously split by several TV aerials. Then she became engulfed in an enormous sweet-bean bun in the shape of a voracious doughnut, a greasy, fragrant vagina liberally sprinkled with crystal sugar. In London, Lorelei had been a member of the Anonymphomaniacs, and even here in Tokyo she kept waking up to intone the therapeutic slogan of the society: 'I am a Nymphomaniac!' It never seemed to do much good, because she was always relapsing. At one point in the night, in a dream of a horde of miniaturized Japanese male members, she had screamed in her sleep: 'Nipponymphomaniacs Unite!' The cheeky little penises had run all over her body like a plague of hairy caterpillars.

A faint rustling sound, in her present state of hyperaesthesia, was enough to rouse her from a dream of being penetrated by one of those giant, coarsely veined penises Hilary had described in Utamaro's *shunga* or 'spring pictures'. Someone was trying to slide *The Nippon News* under her door, without success. Hoping it might be one of those promising bus-boys in bum-freezers, Lorelei leapt out of the sheets and, before she had time to realize she was stark naked, had flung the door open. Outside was the sour-faced desk clerk who had always treated her with such detachment whenever she returned her key, wagging it suggestively. She stood aside and, as goggle-eyed as a slant-eyed oriental can be, he barged into the room,

unzipping himself with fevered gestures as she lay back on the
foot of the bed, ready and willing. 'My first Japanese!' she
breathed, enfolding his business-suited body in her voluptuous
arms. He started groaning and panting in a very convincing
way.

'You have lovely hip! You have big-big-big everywhere. . . .'

Lorelei felt a minor disturbance in the vaginal area, and the
next thing she knew he was zipping himself up and hurrying
out to deliver the rest of his newspapers.

Did he or didn't he? wondered Lorelei. He had left such a
fleeting impression. Checking her receptive areas, she felt a
little sticky substance, but whether it was his or hers she was
incapable of telling. It had all happened so quickly.

'Just in and out, that's Japanese men for you,' she muttered
despondently, peering round the door into the hall to see if
there were any more promising males passing by in a state of
erotic stimulation. But there was no one. She took a shower,
did her hair and make-up and inserted herself into a clinging
black satin sheath dress, black open-work tights and diamanté-
heeled peep-toe shoes. Men, she had discovered, always seemed
to think that women wearing black tights were 'ready for it' – as
she certainly was, after her fruitless flurry with the dismaying
desk clerk.

It was time for breakfast, and she took her usual seat beside
the window looking on to the little garden. In her present
erotomaniac condition, even the bamboos looked manly, and
the tall stone lantern, however tottery, positively phallic. As
she toyed with her sugary scrambled eggs, she mused: I
shouldn't mind being a man, if only women weren't so awful.
This uncalled-for thought left her bewildered. Where had it
come from? How could she, a grown girl, think such a thing
about her own sex? 'Perhaps I'm "bi",' she said to herself,
casting an alluring glance at the little waitress, who went into
a state of shock. She remembered the slogans of the self-help
society called Bisexuals Ambidexterous, with its headquarters
at Clapham Junction: *Bi is Best! Eat your cake and have it! Be 'Bi'
and get the Best of Both!* Then she suddenly felt dizzy. Her head
began to swim, and the little vase with its simple-minded flower
arrangement on her table toppled over.

The little waitress, her face crimson – was it with mirth or embarrassment? – came hurtling in from the kitchen, pointing to the ceiling. Lorelei looked up and saw that the hanging light fittings were swaying from side to side like pendulums. Yet she could feel no gust of wind, which alone could have caused such a phenomenon. But then she felt the floor under her feet shake and squirm. Her chair shuddered, and as she looked out of the window she saw the rickety stone lantern slowly topple over with a dull thud, in a great cloud of dust. Her chandelier earrings were swinging!

The other guests were taking refuge under their tables. The young *maître d'hôtel* came dashing in with a cushion over his head. 'It is earthquake!' he shouted smilingly to Lorelei. 'Be under table with me.' He seized her hand and dived with her under a long serving table with very solid legs, draped with a capacious linen table-cloth. Underneath, there were some empty beer crates and a lot of square, flat cushions. The young man flung her on the cushions and jammed one of them on her head. She was vexed to have her careful morning coiffure deranged, but this was no time for fussing about friseurs, because the head waiter thrust himself on top of her recumbent form, panting: 'You OK me, I protect you. Something hit my backside first, not you on bosom.'

Lorelei, between shudders that rattled the cutlery on the table-top and sent piles of plates crashing to the floor, could feel the panic thudding of the young man's heart as he pressed himself to her, and she clung to him in a delirium of both fright and sexual frenzy. He was just a young boy, really. But he was made like a man. She could feel his generous equipment stiffening against her yielding pelvic basin. Fortunately, she had not put on any panties for breakfast, preferring to let the cool air of morning play between her overheated thighs. Her black satin sheath frock was being pushed up around her hips as she felt herself sliding partly off the collapsing heap of slippery cushions which nevertheless left her intimate parts advantageously elevated, preparatory to penetration. The earthquake's series of tremors seemed to be subsiding, so if she were to take advantage of its bumps and grinds she would have to avail herself as best she could of the consequent after-shocks, unpredictable as they were. Her hand deftly unzipped the youth, but her fingers found themselves lost in a maze of foreign underwear, within which, like some holy infant in swaddling bands, his precious prick was convulsively pulsing. Hauling down his trousers with practised art, she almost groaned in despair. He was wearing knee-length nylon drawers, under which was a pair of Y-fronts, under which was a tightly furled breech-clout or *fundoshi* – in this dire extremity, the lovely word flashed across her mind from the Major's conversation.

It was impossible, in that restricted space, to disentangle his treasure, so as after-shock followed after-shock she groped his balls and his engorged juicer as he began to squirm and pant until she was shaken by something more than a final series of after-shocks of diminishing intensity. He had come in his *fundoshi*. In an irresistible surge of sexual abandon he crushed her in his arms, and thus locked together they rolled to one side, bringing down the hanging table-cloth and the entire breakfast paraphernalia around them. While they disentangled themselves from the steaming mess of coffee, fruit salad and scrambled eggs, they had time to adjust their apparel as the other guests and the waitresses emerged from under the other tables, some of them looking distinctly white around the gills.

The young head waiter helped her to her feet, uttering that well-known cliché, the line he must have heard in a hundred American war movies in the scenes after bombardments, 'Are you all right?'

'Well, in one sense, yes. In another, not at all,' sighed Lorelei, gazing with regret at his flies' flattening protruberance.

'All over now,' he said, smiling a dazzling smile.

'Yes, I'm sure it is,' replied Lorelei, dimpling at his detumescence.

'Now change clothes goodbye *sayonara*.'

He dashed away, leaving Lorelei to pick her way among scattered debris to the elevator. But it had been stopped by the quake. She had to walk upstairs.

✳ 8 : Finding an Apartment

✳ It had, after all that fuss, been a comparatively minor earthquake of a lesser intensity, the kind that shook the islands of Japan fairly frequently. Back in her room, Lorelei divested herself of her sticky sheath and torn tights, and switched on the TV, where an imperturbable announcer was delivering information about the quake: a diagram showed that it had been a mere 4 on the Richter Scale. But Lorelei felt as if she had been through a major upheaval, a medley of conflicting excitations which in the end had left her as frustrated and dissatisfied as ever. Not much damage had been done, in more senses than one.

Lorelei dawdled her way through an hypnotic cigarette, lightly etherized, and began to feel a little better. She languidly showered again, powdering herself all over and generously perfuming her pulse points until she was a walking mist of expensive, body-heated scent. She took care to put on a pair of pink mink panties that she had been cooling in the mini-fridge, and a pair of girlish white knee-socks. She was going to wear her Macleod tartan kilt with a cashmere twin set and – no, she had no pearls, but was hoping some kind person would notice the lack and treat her to some of Nippon's celebrated cultured ones. She put her hair in order, adopting a rather severe practical arrangement, suitable for visiting house agents and inspecting apartments.

The Major was late: he had been delayed by the quake, which had temporarily stopped all the subway trains. He had had to stand in a jam-packed subway carriage for about twenty minutes.

'No hardship, darling. It made my day before it had started!'

He, too, was soberly attired, all in black velvet with mother-of-pearl buttons, some of them in the most unexpected places. There was a row of them stitched down the outside of his flies, though as he had a zip they were strictly non-functional.

'Just eye-catchers, dear,' he explained to Lorelei, who was trying in vain to undo them. 'They've baffled more than one exploring hand.'

He was not sporting a monocle this time but a pair of simply enormous, round, tinted glasses in amber frames, with a matching amber chain slung from their extremities round his fashionably bottle-shaped shoulders, to prevent them from straying.

'They get *so* forgetful, I have to keep them on a leash.'

His 'contrasting' shirt, however, was a muted gold lamé with a Byronic collar that successfully concealed a neck beginning to wrinkle and a pair of incipient jowls. He was a perfect picture of respectability. Lorelei felt she should 'dress down to him'. But there was no more time to change. They were off to inspect an apartment near Shinjuku, one of Tokyo's best-known cosmopolitan teenage centres.

'Where exactly do you live?' Lorelei asked him as they rode the Marunouchi line from the Vanity Fair to Shinjuku.

'I have a gay little *garçonnière* just off the gorgeous Ginza. It costs the earth, but I have to be near the centre of things. I like to keep my finger on the pulse of the public. And I sometimes enrol promising students fresh off the streets.'

'And offer them special terms?'

'If they deserve them.'

'Hilary, with the salary you're paying me, I can't manage a million yen a month for a two-room apartment and bath.'

'Who said you have to pay a million yen a month? You've been reading those screwball newspaper ads in *The Nippon News*, haven't you? Silly girl! Those are just come-ons for diplomatic missions, business executives whose rent is paid by their companies, or representatives of the British Cultural Society – a band of money-grubbing nincompoops if ever there was one.'

'How much do *you* pay?'

'Money and fair words, darling. I have my little jobs on the side, you know. They bring in a bit extra for the essential luxuries only.'

'What kind of jobs? Can you get me in on it?'

'Ah, that would be telling, Lorelei love.'

* * *

After a change of line, they got off the subway at a stop which
looked no different from any other part of Tokyo. There were
some modern high-rise buildings, a couple of banks, two
department stores, several coffee shops, restaurants and bars.
It might have been anywhere; it had no distinct personality.
Indeed, apart from the many crude advertisements written in
Japanese characters, they might have been in some well-to-do
suburb of London or New York.

The house agent was waiting for them at the east exit to the
station. He was a round, fat gentleman in a crumpled suit and a
rather grubby shirt and tie. His long hair was greasy and he had
a curiously pallid bald spot. He had a permanent moist-lipped
smile showing perfect teeth – real or artificial? Lorelei, even with
her sharp eyes, could not tell. She disliked the obsequious, oily
nature of the man's expression. He introduced himself as Mr
Yamada and handed them his name card, printed in Japanese
on one side, in English on the other.

The Major introduced Lorelei, and many bows were exchanged, while Yamada-san's eyes, half closed with fat, roamed
appreciatively over his new client's voluptuous curves and took
in her shining blonde hair.

'You American girl, yes? Where you from?'

He seemed distinctly disappointed when Lorelei said she was
British.

'You American guy?' Yamada-san asked Hilary, looking
doubtfully at his very un-American appearance. Hilary explained that he, too, was British.

'Ah, so, British genitalman!' Yamada-san squealed like a pig.
'Very goot!'

Yamada-san dissolved into a yapping laugh that soon turned
into a fit of unbridled coughing, after which he hawked loudly
and spat copiously on the pavement. 'Very goot!' he said,
gazing critically at the results of his productive cough. 'I
know many American from base. You know base? Yokosuka?
Yokohama? You know Sergeant Van Allen? He have lovely
wife and kids. . . .'

Chatting in this half-witted way, Yamada-san led them along
some back streets of louche-looking bars, all closed at this early
hour, with big blue plastic bags of garbage outside their doors.

They stopped outside a tall, shabby building.

'Very nice located. This part cheap, so cheap. But many high-class bar, bar madame, nice girl, give you nice massage, all my friend.'

There was no elevator. They toiled up to the fifth floor. Yamada-san unlocked the door and ushered them into a tiny entrance hall, so small that they were all jammed together as in a subway rush-hour. Lorelei felt the house agent's belly shoving against her.

'We take off shoes, yes?'

They removed their shoes and with some difficulty stooped down to slip their stockinged feet into slippers. Yamada-san stepped up into another very confined space.

'Very neat, cosy, very warm all time.'

The Major and Lorelei were still standing in the dark little entry as Yamada-san pointed to his left, sliding a door open to reveal a toilet which was a hole in the floor surrounded by a grimy porcelain oblong with a rounded porcelain hood at one end.

'Japanese toilet, ha-ha. We call *benjo*. Very convenient. I show you.'

Mr Yamada squeezed himself into the narrow toilet and squatted down over the opening. Fortunately, his demonstration did not require the lowering of his pants. He hauled himself to his feet again with some difficulty and worked the flush. Then, sliding open another door, activated a diminutive shower.

'Very nice. Obey call of nature, take shower same time,' he laughed. 'And can answer front-door bell no moving, ha-ha.' His spit flew. 'Very goot!'

He led them into a minuscule kitchen with a sink, a gas ring, a small table and two stools. Next to the kitchen was an even smaller bedroom, three tatami mats in size.

'Nice bedroom for lady, many lovers, good location, near station and many convenience store. Only two hundred thousand yen month. Three month advance, also key money, and small present for owner, one hundred thousand yen for his goodwill. He change light bulb if broken, etcetera etcetera.'

When they added it all up, it came to over one million yen,

just to get into the place. When Lorelei asked if there would be
any refund when she left, Yamada-san, hastily looking at his
wrist-watch, replied: 'You wanna apartment, you no wanna
apartment. I busy man. You not find good place like this,
fucking cheap as shit.'

Both the Major and Lorelei were accustomed to strong
language, but somehow these artless oaths emerging from
that fleshy mouth with its permanently radiant smile sounded
unexpectedly shocking. It was as if Yamada-san did not really
understand the nature of the language he was using with such
haphazard fluency.

'Me many GI customer. GI like me. Many. Call me
Buddy. Good ole Buddy Yamada. You take it you wanna see
another place but lotsa dough?'

In the end, they decided to take it on a temporary basis, until
Lorelei got settled into her job and then had time to shop around
for something better, but not dearer.

Yamada-san seemed very gratified as the Major paid him
cash in ten thousand yen notes.

'I no like American Express card, Visa, Master Card. I lose
many money.'

The contract was signed over a coffee in the nearby Waldolf
Ashtolia (*sic*) coffee shop. Then Yamada-san handed over the
keys, saying: 'It's all yours. Yippee. Take it away. So long, you
guys.'

In a rather depressed silence the Major and Lorelei let
themselves into the apartment. They would have to buy some
pots and pans and other basic necessities, get in bread, coffee,
tea, milk, eggs. That would do for this weekend. The Major
took Lorelei's telephone number. 'First class Monday morning,
nine o'clock,' he sang encouragingly.

Lorelei shuddered.

'I'll call for you at seven-thirty. It's not far – Yoyogi. But there
are the rush-hour crowds to consider.'

'Are you going to leave me here all alone until then?'

'Well, if you like, we could visit a few bars this evening. . . .'

Lorelei agreed to meet Hilary at the station around seven
that evening, which would give her time to do all her shopping
– using body language.

✵ 9 : Gay Bar Blues

✵ 'The Lavender Samurai – What an unusual name for a gay bar!' 'And only a little further on, there's The Jewelled Jockstrap. It's a leather joint. Very aromatic.'

Major Sitfast and Lorelei had set out on a tour of Tokyo bars. First of all the Major was just showing her round. It was still too early for any of the bars to be jumping, or even 'interesting'.

'And this is a lesbian lap of luxury, The Dewy Dildo. Men often find lesbian bars more restful than any other kind.'

'Are they admitted?' Lorelei tried to look puzzled, as she expected this was being demanded of her.

'It depends', Hilary said ambiguously, 'who you're with or if you're alone. Or on the colour of your eyes. A les can be very quirkish, you know.'

'Do I?' rippled Lorelei. 'Look, there's another – Men Only. I presume that's lesbian.'

'Correct. And here's Kimono Cruelty – disappointingly gentle in its severity.'

'And Fundoshi Fascination – back to the boys, obviously.'

'Yes, dear. They are the ones who put the "fun" in *fundoshi*.'

There were quite a number, too, with literary names: Come with the Wind, Maupassant, Daddy Long Legs, Lady Murasaki, Jack Rondon, Genet and Sunset Mum.

'These are for gay intellectuals – artists, writers . . .'

'Who on earth is Sunset Mum?'

'Somerset Maugham *à la japonaise*. And Grim Grin is Graham Greene.'

'Here's The House of Lords.'

'Very popular with certain members of the Diet. Isn't that too, too British?'

'You know I make a point of never being surprised at anything. Ours is such a common House of Commons.'

They had turned off Kabukicho into a main street, filled mostly with teenage punks and motor-cycle gangs on thigh-stretching Kawasakis and Hondas. Despite their sequinned helmets, the bikers seemed terribly tame, and the punks were very ordinary grotesques. Lots of the youths were very tall and excessively skinny, with pallid, petulant faces overshadowed by unreal-looking post-Presley forelocks or pompadours.

When Lorelei commented on this phenomenon, the Major informed her that many of the younger generation had been brought up on instant ramen and noodles, hamburgers, fried chicken and other junk foods.

'They are referred to as overgrown leeks. But the ones in the fancy dress doing those very boring repetitive dances are from the Harajuku area, and they're called *takénoko* – *four* syllables, please – which means "bamboo shoots".'

'How very vegetable.'

For her evening out, Lorelei had donned one of her most fetching outfits, a sleeveless, tight-fitting cheongsam of white kid leather hand embossed with golden chrysanthemums arranged in a seductively asymmetrical eccentric pattern so that each chrysanthemum drew attention (by being situated just off them) to the basic components of the female form. She was heavily hung with large home-made beads, long loops of them hanging below her twinkling, triangular knees. She was wearing the new 'fairylight' tights woven with hundreds of the weeniest electric coloured lights which, attached to a wisp of a battery tucked into her pink mink panties, kept flashing on and off in a languorous aleatory rhythm.

Major Hilary Sitfast had decided to go military and had put on his old Grenadier Guards uniform, simply dripping with costume jewellery and behung with epaulettes and the medals of two world wars in the most unexpected places. But instead of a bearskin he wore a diamanté tiara with large fake jewels looking like Stop, Caution, Go traffic signals. They made a striking couple, but in that atmosphere of tinselly extravaganza and malevolent masquerade, their uniqueness went unnoticed. They both wore lipstick in very pale tones of purple and black, which made them look as if they had been sucking indelible pencils. '"Our lips are not

so black as they are painted,"' quoted Hilary. They had
helped to make each other up, so both had amaranthine
touches of eye-shadow, and of course those fascinating
new chenille eyelashes whose furry fans appeared to flog
faintly the air of spring. The Major had had to abandon
his monocles in order to accommodate them. They turned
Lorelei's drenched violet eyes into wondering anemones
('wine-dark', she called them, having flipped through a
Penguin Homer while waiting for her flight to be called at
Heathrow).

They turned off into a narrow side-street emblazoned with
the signs of a thousand 'snacks' or 'members bars' (not
what one might hope them to be) and another sprinkling of
alternative taverns.

'Oh, look!' exclaimed the Major. 'There's the Brutish Cunts
All – the favourite gay hang-out of the British Cultural Society
and, if I'm not mistaken, there is one of its representatives being
flung out on his arse.'

The person who had been thrown out, an elderly littérateur
with a distinct resemblance to Oscar Wilde in his final days,
managed to pick himself up and hobble painfully away,
followed by an ingratiating pimp offering 'nice boy, Blitish
genitalman?'

'Let's go in and see what he's been up to,' giggled the Major.
But as they advanced towards the bar, the reason became
evident. There was a notice on the door, saying *Japanese Only.
No Aids is Good Aids.*

'What does it mean?'

'Alack,' sighed the Major, his gilt and crystal epaulettes all a-
tremble, 'they think all Westerners have Aids. To them, we're
all Rock Hudsons. A number of Japanese gays have been found
to have the disease, and indeed there have been some deaths.
But many of the cases have been hushed up. It is inconceivable
to them that the vaunted homogenic purity of Japanese blood
should be sullied by foreign transfusions. So the Japanese gays
have outlawed foreign homos, and most of us are not welcome
even in those bars and baths so noted for their foreign clientele
– once a powerful attraction for boys on the make. Thank God
we've not yet been banned from teaching.'

Lorelei, after a long afternoon of buying futon, fruit and bits of cardboard furniture, as well as a lamp fitting in the shape of an alabaster piss-pot, was beginning to feel both hungry and thirsty. So they entered a restaurant serving tempura, or fried seafood and vegetables. The young eels were particularly tasty, they were told, so they ordered a plateful, but were horrified at the spectacle of them being eviscerated alive on the counter before their very eyes. The cook would hold down the wriggling elver with one hand and transpierce its head with a skewer held in the other, then with a fine knife rip open the body and zip out the entire spine. Then the poor creature would be chopped into short lengths, which even then continued twitching before they were dipped into batter and fried. Even the bones were fried. 'Calcium,' explained the athletic youth who performed these complex operations with an artistry that took away some of the unpleasantness of the sight.

They had drunk a couple of bottles of sake. But after that exhibition Lorelei felt she needed something stronger – a violet *crème de menthe*, which is a Japanese speciality. They were fortunate to find a gay bar, wittily named Up and Coming, whose door bore the words, in English, *Foreigners bring own glass. Aids prevention*. They nipped into a china store and bought a couple of tumblers, and thus equipped were allowed to enter the bar. But it was an extremely boring place. All the Japanese huddled at one end of the counter, visibly ostracizing our benighted pair. Lorelei was beginning to feel desperate. When, oh when would she get her hands on a real man? Would she have to wait until Monday, when her first classes began? She got rather distressingly drunk, and the Major had to see her home.

※ 10 : Coffee Shop Conspiracies

※ As soon as he had seen Lorelei tucked safely into bed, and after having deposited a chaste kiss on her limp wrist as she drifted off into sleep, Major Hilary Sitfast hurriedly walked a few blocks to where he had a secret *pied-à-terre*, a tiny cupboard of a room rented from the grandmother of one of his former pupils, Hideki, a promising female impersonator.

The Major had his own key, so there was no need to disturb the old granny, who acted as caretaker in the house inherited by Hideki from his former lover, the late kabuki actor known to his intimates as Kiki de Toshimaku.

Hilary used the little room to store some of his erotic magazines and part of his wardrobe. Here he divested himself of his fanciful get-up and removed his make-up. Then he hung up the Grenadier Guards uniform carefully in a herb-scented plastic bag, and slipped into a pair of worn jeans and a black sweater. Putting on a black nylon wig and dark glasses, he was transformed into a Japanese in all but speech. He got over this difficulty by carrying with him a card that announced, in several languages, *I am deaf and dumb. Please use body language.*

Thus attired, the Major, completely at ease in his new role, walked with a firm step towards the station. It was now nearly midnight and there were not so many people about. He got on an overhead train which took him a few stops to a district known as the 'students' quarter', Kanda, where there were many bookstores, both learned and pornographic, and several colleges and universities. During his brief train trip, he was accosted by one or two revolting drunks, reeking of cheap whisky and sake. The Major ignored their advances. When he got out of the train, the platform was starred with great splurges of vomit. They seemed to be a mixture of beer, whisky, curry rice, seaweed and bright-red bits of pickle, a

colour combination curiously reminiscent of the Burberry
'club check'. Hilary allowed himself a fastidious shudder.
The bookstores were closed and shuttered, and the universities were dark. The dome of the Nikolai Cathedral of
the Greek Orthodox Church, named after its founder, the
mysterious Russian priest Ioan Kasatkin Nikolai, and designated by the Government's Ministry of Cultural Affairs as an
'Important Cultural Property', soared above Meiji, Nihon and
Chuo Universities. To the Major, Japanese universities were
something of a joke: students usually did not go there to study
but to enjoy a four-year vacation after the rigours of school life
and before the even greater rigours of the professional, social
and family rat-race that would occupy the rest of their days. In
a Japanese university, nearly everyone is allowed to graduate:
hundreds of thousands of more or less ignorant graduates are
released every spring from the diploma mills, as the mammoth
universities of Japan are called. The Major often wondered
how on earth Japan had become so commercially successful,
given the poor quality of her university graduates, who spent
most of their time reading comics and playing games. He had
come to the conclusion that in Japan it is better not to be too
intelligent, the more easily to fit into the mass. Then, once
employed, one is quietly swept along to retirement on the
system that guarantees jobs for life, however incompetent one
may be – there is always some superior with a little extra
knowledge and experience to correct one's mistakes.

The worst part of life for a Japanese is childhood. A boy or
a girl starts preparing at the age of three for the seemingly
unending series of tests and examinations that will bring them
to their final goal, around the age of eighteen – entrance into
some university, the more prestigious the better. It is hard
to enter a top-class university, whose graduates get the best
positions; but once enrolled in such an institution one can
more or less relax for the rest of one's days. Nobody fails: the
consensus society in which the stronger support the weaker
brethren does not admit failure.

There were one or two noodles-stalls with a few belated
customers slurping hot, steaming noodles. But the Major made
for a small coffee shop which was open until midnight. It had a

Russian name. The Major entered its dim, smoky atmosphere. There was a small counter, and six or seven booths decorated with silver-birch logs and cheap balalaikas. Russian folk-songs were coming from the Muzak.

A young waiter in a peasant shirt girded with a wide leather belt which showed off his supple loins came to take the Major's order.

'Ko-hee-o kudasai,' Hilary said with a smile.

'You want coffee?' the blank-looking waiter asked unnecessarily.

'Yes, dear,' the Major pettishly replied. His disguise had been penetrated.

'One hotto!'

As the youth shouted the order for a hot coffee and walked towards the counter where another youth was serving drinks, the Major mused appreciatively on his waiter's neat little posterior, encased in worn black velvet corduroy. Really, fancy not understanding his immaculate Japanese – just about the only phrase he could utter correctly too! Sometimes, Hilary thought, the Japanese were not switched on. Not on the same wavelength. Their minds were usually far away on something else, some remote day-dream. So much so, that many of them, expecting to hear a foreigner speak English, failed to comprehend even the best speakers of Japanese. It was one of the results of Japanese education, which is all rote learning and repetition: they are never taught to listen, only to bellow useless phrases, preferably as loudly as possible, through a mike. The Major sighed. The inability of his pupils to listen to what he was saying was one of the great problems he faced in his teaching. However, if they were taught properly at school, he would have no pupils. So it was all for the best, really.

The Major sipped his black, bitter coffee meditatively. There were only one or two customers sitting on stools at the counter, waiting for the last train to the suburbs.

After a few minutes the door opened and an elegant young lady in a kimono entered and sat in the booth next to Hilary's. She was exquisite. But after a fleeting glance, the drunks at the counter ignored her. She ordered a glass of Russian tea and then sat with eyes modestly downcast, occasionally patting

the entrancing wisps of hair on her delicate nape. She was
sitting with her back to the Major, and he admired the way
the collar of her rather sober spring kimono hung down
at the back, exposing the back of her neck, that part of a
woman's body which Japanese men find most enticing. A
faint perfume wafted from her, a mingled scent of camellia
oil lightly applied to her hair and eyebrows, and of the latest
creation from the laboratories of a famous male dress designer,
'Princess Diana'. She neatly adjusted her kimono opening over
non-existent breasts.

When she had sipped her tea, the girl got up and went to the
toilet at the back of the coffee shop. She was there for only a few
moments, then came out and paid her bill before leaving.

As soon as she had left, the Major went to the toilet. There,
on a ledge next to a rather stagnant flower arrangement, lay a
large manila envelope. The Major seized it and quickly stuffed
it up his jumper. Then, just as he was alout to leave the toilet,
the door opened and his waiter looked in.

'Oh, sorry.'

'That's all right, dear. Come on in.'

'You want boy tonight? You want me?'

'What time do you finish work?'

'Soon. I part-time student, doing side-job. No class
tomorrow.'

'All right. What's your name?'

'Kenji. Call me Ken.'

'I'll wait for you at the corner – Kenji.'

He was not, Hilary decided, as dumb as he looked. Yes,
he was certainly switched on – at least in one direction.
Promising. . . . And he had obviously never heard of Aids.
Not that he had anything to fear from the Major, who as as
pure as driven snow.

✺ 11 : Sir Paul and the Hun

✺ In a smart, de-luxe penthouse in Azabu, the society cesspool of Tokyo, Sir Paul Pinker, director of the British Cultural Society, was trying to recover from the rude fall upon his coccyx inflicted upon him by the brutal bouncer at the British Cunts All gay bar. He was lying on a diplomatic tiger-skin naked as the day he was born (which was not yesterday) and having his rear end massaged ever so gently by his houseboy, Taro, an energetic youth (he had to be) from the Waseda University Rugby Club. He was employed full time by Sir Paul, with time off once a week for academic studies, which consisted mainly of Rugby training followed by ribald geisha songs and supermanly larks in the showers.

'Oh, Ta-Ta!' – as Sir P. P. affectionately dubbed his gentleman's gentleman. 'You really are a treasure, worth every yen of the vast sums I lay out on you. Ooh! Naughty!'

Taro's wicked middle finger had slipped, giving his master a moderate thrill.

'But sir,' simpered tough young Taro, 'soon I will graduate, when you have finished writing for me my thesis on *Rebecca of Sunnybrook Farm*, then I must go out into the wide, cruel world and work for Mitsubishi and get a wife and all that shit.'

His English was of unusual fluency through his almost hourly contact with the top banana of the Society of St George. And it was a British Oxford accent that only he and his employer could understand. Whenever Sir Paul consented to give a public lecture on 'Some Unusual Aspects of Edmund Blunden' or 'My Literary Life at Oxford – A Nest of Singing Nerds', his Japanese audience – two or three if he was lucky – would sit spellbound by incomprehension, and by his curious gesture of hoisting his balls with a free hand from time to time. They supposed it to be a British upper-class habit, but were sadly disappointed by the impression it produced when they imitated it on their student exchange programme visits to England, on BCS bursaries of course.

'Don't you worry your little head about that, Ta-Ta. I'll see you right.'

'But sir, the final examinations!'

An expression of frozen horror passed over Taro's rather elementary features. Sir Paul was fond of rough trade, provided it was not *too* rough, not *too* Neanderthal. . . . But *pretty* boys were anathema to him.

'I have my little plan, dear,' said Sir P, turning over with some difficulty and plunging Taro's dangling prick into his flaccid mouth. There were some moments of silence, broken only by gasps and gurgles from Sir Paul, and groans of simulated rapture from Taro, who had been sucked off already once that evening and felt his employer was demanding a bit too much, expecting him to come again within the hour.

'Plan, sir?'

Sir Paul, invariably referred to as 'Sir Pinker' in the American press, gave up trying to flog a dead horse, and sat up.

'Yes, Ta-Ta. Before your final exams, I'm going to give you a little private tuition.'

Oh, great gods of Nippon, thought Taro to himself. Not that again!

For Sir P was from time to time inclined to 'discipline' his houseboy in the manner he had learnt to love at Eton. And then Taro, naked but for a BA gown and mortar-board, had to inflict it upon his boss. Of course it all ended in passionate embraces and the singing of 'The Eton Boating Song' with a background provided by the Band of the Royal Fusiliers recorded on *karaoke* tape.

There came a subdued tinkling of fairy-bell chimes.

'Oh God, that must be Hunter Elvet already! Bring me my robe, make yourself decent, and go and answer the bloody door.'

Hunter Elvet was Sir P's 'opposite number', though rather lower in the social scale, at the American Boys' Club, for male traffic orphans, one of the many cultural and charitable works of the CIA. It was well known as a hotbed of vice, and a prominent and successful training-ground for youthful *agents provocateurs*. Many a government of the First, Second and even Third Worlds, not to mention United Nations secretariat, had been brought down through its representatives' lustful indiscretions with some underprivileged traffic orphan. And Hunter Elvet hand-picked them for his own personal training methods.

He was a tall, lugubrious, Fulbright Scholar type, with the air of a defrocked gay Unitarian clergyman. Attired all in black, the only 'point of colour' about him was the crimson rosette of the Order of the Protestant Patriots, which toned in with his long, mean nose. He spoke fluent Japanese with that peculiar Japanese fluency which is like a tap left running all night long. Prattle, prattle, prattle. . . . He had been born and bred in Japan, where his father, and his grandfather before him, had been missionaries dedicated to the cause of clothing the Japanese in Christian long johns instead of those disgustingly revealing *fundoshi*. Just another example of how religion takes all the joy out of human existence.

'Am I early?' he asked, extending a chill, skeletal hand to Taro, who managed to ignore it by bowing deeply, so deeply he could see a liberal scattering of dandruff on Elvet-san's flies.

'Not at all, Hunter dear,' came the honeyed tones of Sir Paul from the living-room. It was a 'restful' room, all in brown velvet and olde-worlde tapestry cushions, ordered by the Embassy direct from Mapleton's. The unusual number of pink-shaded standard lamps suggested a domestic drama on the stage of some third-rate provincial repertory theatre. *The Constant Nymph*, perhaps, or *Rebecca*.

'It's the privilege of royalty to be always dead on time,' cooed Sir P. 'But I don't see why lesser mortals shouldn't enjoy it too.'

'My dear,' whinnied Hunter, sometimes known as 'the Hun', 'don't say "dead on time" like that, it's too much like "dead on arrival" or DOA, and my nerves won't stand it.'

'You poor dear! You *are* in a state. Let me get you a drink. The usual?'

'A double.'

Sir Paul made a jug of his famous cocktail, the Blue Gin, which was composed entirely of British Beefeater gin and 'just a dash of Waterman's', as Sir P was fond of saying. It had once won first

prize as the Literary Cocktail of the Year during his stint with
the BSC in Kuala Lumpur.

'Now then, Hunny, calm down and tell nursey all about it.'

'Well, my Tomohiro – such an attractive boy when I picked
him up at the Orphanage for the Children of Traffic Accident
Victims Extraordinary' (known by the convenient acronym of
OCTAVE). 'And kind and loving, even if he does do it only
for the money. But honestly, my dear, the *shock* – I gave him ten
thousand yen, which is being on the generous side for orphans,
even these days, which he said he needed for a facial and a
haircut. Well, he came back one week later with the whole
of his left shoulder and upper arm tattooed with such a *loud*
design of peonies and a leaping carp. Real *yakuza* style! It's
simply revolting, but I can't stop it, because I can't do without
him. I'm crazy about the lad, and he knows it. And every time
we have sex in the steam-room I just have to give him a few
thousand for his bus-fare back to the Orphanage.'

Hunny took a big gulp of his cocktail, which was turning his
lips and tongue a heart-attack blue. Silently he held out his glass
for another.

'Now, every time he comes back to service me, he comes
with yet another section of his anatomy tattooed. My spies
have told me he sits in that gay public bath for hours. Says it
improves the colours, though I know for certain he's only there
to pick up customers. And he gets them, mainly minor officials
from the embassies, English conversation teachers from Tokyo
University and so on – that is, the dregs of foreign fairydom.'

'My dear, how appallingly disloyal!' murmured Sir Paul,
with unctuous commiseration that barely concealed the spiteful
ecstasy of *schadenfreude*.

'I know *I* didn't pay for that crude snake he's had done twining
round his left leg and sticking its head in where he won't allow
me to put so much as the tip of my pinky.'

'Dear boy, that's nothing,' crowed Paul Pinker. 'One of my
boys has been getting tattooed all over for years, and there isn't
an inch of natural skin left on him. He even had a couple of
butterflies tattooed on his glans penis, and a number of cultured
pearls surgically inserted into the skin of the main shaft. They
do produce the most stimulating effect, I must say. But he's

such a remarkable phenomenon that the Japanese Government has designated him as what they call "an intangible cultural property". So now he won't let me lay a finger on him. And he once was so very, *very* tangible.'

'Well, there are fortunately plenty of other fish in the Sea of Japan,' sighed Hunter, 'if only one can get one's hands on them. Recently all the boys are becoming very wary of foreigners, even for just a one-night stand. It's the Aids menace, of course. But it's also the rising prosperity and independence of the young in this baby-boomer youth culture. They've never had it so good, so why should they bother with us poor foreign queens?'

'Only a few years ago they were all moaning about their inferiority complex. Of course some of them really were inferior, so there was nothing very surprising in that. But today even the inferior ones are developing a superiority complex. I suppose it's part of the nationalist trend.'

'As Seidensticker so truly said, the Japanese are good only in adversity. In defeat and poverty. Once they begin to recover, they get above themselves.'

'Well, I think that view is a teeny bit extreme,' mused Sir Paul in his round-table seminar manner. 'Seidensticker is American, after all. The Yanks do tend to go to extremes, though not as maniacally far as the Japanese, whose culture and educational system, it seems to me, have much in common with the Russia of the tsars, which is more or less the Russia of today.'

'I think I need another of your Blue Funks.'

'Thank goodness we don't care for the stronger sex.' Paul tried to pour the drink without shuddering too much. 'Once a Japanese woman gets her claws into a foreigner. . . . Remember poor Algernon Acton? Such a nice, clean-living boy, might have been mistaken for a Mormon, really. That gruesome geisha who bemused him with her itsy-bitsy parlour games, blind-man's buff in the nude and all that infantile entertainment. . . . The suicide threats *and* attempts began daily when he tried, so gently, to get disentangled.'

Acton, an upright young New Zealander, a rising diplomatic star, had been practically devoured alive by an aging, wealthy geisha – one of the many perils in learning to speak Japanese too well. In the end, she had inveigled him into a double suicide.

Tying themselves together with her brocade sash, they had hurled themselves into a lake of boiling mud at a famous hot-spring resort in Hokkaido. A year later, their bodies, still enlaced but completely fossilized, were on display at a local museum of natural history.

'*So* silly to get worked up to that point,' Hunny moaned. 'He was really one of *us*, you know. I made him once when he was drunk at those steam baths in Ikebukuro, after a tedious New Year party at the Embassy, where we had to play postman's knock with the International Ladies' Flower Arrangement Group. If he'd only admitted it to himself, all that need never have happened. And he could have had any of us, because, my dear, he was *very* well hung. Ah, those rugger toughs! Those divine All-Blacks!'

'All the woes in the world come from people getting all worked up and dramatic. In Japan today everything's a TV "home drama".' Paul yawned at the mere thought of the abysmal banalities of Japanese television. His own set was permanently veiled by a curtain of rare Chinese embroidered silk. 'People are such sentimental fools. It's also partly the pernicious influence of the cinema close-up. People now tend to see themselves and their emotions constantly in close-up. An actor has only to blink in order to produce an emotional cataclysm. And the Japanese are so very impressionable. Their favourite answer, when you ask them their opinion about something, is "I was deeply impressed." I ask you . . .'

'I'm beginning to feel a little better,' smiled Hunny, reaching for his fifth Blue Gin.

'I only wish I were,' pouted Sir Paul. 'Next week I've got to go and give my 349/B/CN/PP lecture at the Tosh Hall in Hibiya, on "British Culture Learns to Live with the Bomb".'

'My dear, such terribly sincere titles you think up. I'll never forget your "British Economic Flowering in the Potteries".'

'Ah yes, that's my No. 8/PNG/249/X/PP. I wowed them with it in Wakayama. There's no captive audience like the Japanese one. They adore being lectured. They'll sit and listen for hours to the most boring drivel, if only it's in English, even when they don't understand it.'

'I might say, especially when they don't understand it.'

'And especially when it's under the aegis of our British
Cultural Society. I might do one for your place on "The Close-
up in the Japanese Cinema". I hope they don't misunderstand
the title – it's not about groping boys at the back of the gay
movie-houses.'
They both burst into hysterical laughter.
'I might take it down to our Kyoto branch later,' mused Sir P.
'Then I could get extra expenses, staying overnight at a luxury
hotel, but actually putting myself up at our local representative's
mansion. And I could visit all those craft shops and get lots of free
gifts – dolls, brocades, etcetera etcetera.'
'Well, you can do one for us, if you let me do one for you. Fair's
fair. We also like to make a little on the side, you know. And what
with my present expenses for Tomohiro . . .'
'It's a deal. And I'll get you invited down to Kyoto to give
your usual Longfellow lecture. You can stay at our rep's –
Fanny Alexander's quite an astute middle-aged queen, with
quite a court of beautiful boys.'
'We have to be careful whom we invite to lecture at our
American Boys' Club. You wouldn't *believe* what these naïve
performance artists get up to! We think it best to stick to
linguistics and – but very tricky in these days of trade friction
– economics. Linguistic specialists are always reliable, and the
Japanese can cope with a foreign language when it's reduced to
a sort of algebraic system.'
'I could hardly agree more,' opined Sir Paul. 'I know just what
you have to go through. Artists, writers, actors – the *state* they
arrive in for their "lectures", as they call them – drunk, dirty,
drugged, dishevelled, in the throes of some sordid passion. I shall
never forget that awful poetess, whom we had done *everything* for,
in the way of pushing her books, getting her grants, exposing
her name, her photo in all the papers, her titmouse voice on
record at the BCS Libraries, and then she starts undressing in
front of her audience!'
'And Japanese students are *so* prudish,' the Hun regretted.
'It's the missionary influence in their universities.'
Oh well, one more *persona non grata* for our confidential files. I
hear – but *don't* pass this on, unless you simply must – that she
has some curious malformation of the clitoris.'

'Who on earth told you that?'

'Oh, one of our little spies. Good-looking Goro, you know, angelic face really, and quite all right in *that* department when I tested him out. We call him our *enfant provocateur* and use him to keep visiting British females happy. The men, too, enjoy his Japandrogynous gifts and favours. And he reports to us on any abnormalities of behaviour we might not already know about from our secret reports. We don't want any *degenerates* working for us, you know.'

'Quite. We do seem to get the dregs of the literary world in Japan.'

'Well, I must go and dust my thighs with Johnson's Baby Powder. If I don't take this precaution, lecturing always brings me out in a heat-rash.'

'You poor darling. A woman's work is never done.'

'Yes, I've not had a minute to myself since I arrived at the office at noon. I had my half-hour with *The Times* and then it was time for a few drinks, then lunch until three-thirty, then sign a few letters and back home by five in time for the Happy Hour. A stroll around some of the hot spots, a little contretemps at the Brutish Cunts All, then a restorative drink or two, dinner, and my "Time with Taro", as I call it.'

'By the way, dear, would you mind if . . .'

'Not at all. He's available until midnight. I should warn you, though, he's already come once and half tonight. But he should have recovered by now. Taro, Ta-Ta! Customer! Give him ten thousand. . . .'

✳ 12 : Gilded Youth

✳Hideki Matsumoto and Major Hilary Sitfast called on Lorelei Thrillingly in the afternoon of her first day at the little apartment. They had already lunched, but she, barely recovered from her hangover of the night before, breakfasted on canned soup and an apple. So now she felt ready to face Tokyo again. She was sipping her third black coffee.

Hideki was a charming young female impersonator who had been the favourite pupil of another master in the genre, Kiki de Toshimaku, recently deceased. The latter had died of a heart attack while being rogered by a sumo wrestler in a private bathroom at the Mauve Chrysanthemum Sauna, a popular rendezvous for Japanese men, both hets and homos. 'Japanese Only', of course.

This afternoon Hideki was in a light spring kimono with an overall design of cherry blossoms, and his *obi* or sash of brilliant brocade was decorated with embroidered fans. On his feet were sparkling white *tabi*, or sock-shoes. In the divisions between the big toes and the rest he delicately gripped the lizard-skin thongs of his pearly *geta*, or sandals. A pastel-tinted swansdown stole covered his gently sloping shoulders, for though it was spring, the late afternoons could turn chilly.

An acute observer would at once have noticed that Hideki (whose feminine name was Fumiko) was none other than the mysterious kimonoed creature who had left the large manila envelope in the toilet of the Russian coffee shop the night before. . . .

By contrast, the Major and Lorelei were very subdued. Hilary was still wearing his dark outfit of the previous evening, though he had removed his black nylon wig, releasing fragile amber curls to the petal-snowed breezes. Lorelei, for a wonder, was all in black. Quoting Firbank, she groaned: '"I see life today in the colour of mould . . .'"

'But black suits you,' Hideki assured her. 'And it's the height of fashion.'

'In Japan, but nowhere else,' snapped the Major.

But of course Lorelei still sported her diamond chandelier earrings – 'When at home, do as the homos do.'

'You sound a trifle bitter today, Lorelei dear. Feeling liverish?'

But Lorelei was simply sexually frustrated. Perhaps this afternoon's little outing would produce some satisfying masculine response – and by that she did not mean getting felt up on a bus or a train.

They took a taxi to Harajuku, which on Sundays was the centre of life for all the gilded youth of the capital. There in the park they could observe the younger generation at play, from the age of twelve onwards up to no more than seventeen. There were crowds of young people in absurd make-up and outrageous costumes, dancing – or rather jumping – to the belting beat of monotonous heavy rock. They mostly just jigged up and down on the spot, as if on pogo sticks. They were watched by hundreds of tourists, many of them foreign, which seemed to put added zest into their gyrations.

'They love being gaped at, the centre of attention,' Hideki explained to Lorelei, who at once felt herself becoming a prey to creeping boredom. 'You see, they've been coddled by their mothers all their lives. The real world, after all that petting, is just too hard to take. So they escape in fantasy, and wear comic clothes – just another kind of conformity, really. The make-up and hair-styles are post-punk or late Elvis Presley. There are no Mods and Rockers here, no riots. It's all very ordinary.'

Hideki's English was fluent and correct nearly all the time. He had been brought up in a diplomatic family and had lived most of his life in English-speaking parts of the world. But he liked to affect a Japanese accent, addressing Lorelei as 'Rolerei' and Hilary as 'Hiraly'. Sometimes he called the former by her family name, the better to enjoy his artificial lambdacisms and rhotacisms in Thrillingly, which he pronounced 'Flirringry', with a big, poofy 'F'.

'What are those girls doing behind the bushes?' Lorelei asked hopefully, drawing her companions in the direction of a small clump of azaleas.

'They are changing their clothes, darling,' said the Major. 'They come here wearing the customary black school uniform – long gym-dress, middy blouse and sailor collar, and change into their Harajuku outfits, transforming themselves, unknown to their parents, into these colourful bamboo shoots, or *takénoko*. Well, it's certainly a welcome change from all the blackness!'

As they approached the bushes, the girls started screaming and giggling with hands over mouths, flashing their pristine white cotton panties as they struggled into their complicated fancy dress. One of the girls shouted 'Peeper' as Lorelei looked over the low hedge. The Major and Hideki had turned their faces away from the (to them) revolting spectacle of female adolescent nudity.

'Be careful, dear,' the Major admonished Lorelei. 'Some of them have been known to call the police.'

'But peeping is such a common sport everywhere in Tokyo,' said Hideki. 'There are always photographers snapping courting couples in Hibiya Park and Shinjuku Gyoen and other public places. The Japanese have a peeping Tom mentality, as can be seen from their weekly scandal magazines, and especially from the disgusting *HoKus PoKus* which invades the private lives of every personality in the news or on TV. And at night the public parks are full of "peepers and feelers", creeping round the benches and the bushes, getting as close to dating couples as possible, watching the full sexual act, and even taking part in it. Many couples go to the parks hoping for a peeper and a feeler to stimulate their jaded passions. And the peepers and feelers know it. Often the girl does not know who has fucked her, or the man who has sucked him.'

'Really!' Lorelei cried rather breathlessly, filing away the information in her memory bank and determining to become a 'peeper and feeler' herself at the earliest opportunity. This sounded like a better sort of fun than packed trains or groovy movie-house gropes.

'What about these gay movie-houses one reads about in all the best guide books?' she inquired. 'Do they admit women?'

Hideki and the Major looked at one another.

'Not officially, darling,' said the Major. 'But women do sometimes manage, in the guise of men, to insinuate themselves into the standees behind the back rows. They usually wear men's garments, or, at the New Year season, men's kimonos. Or they dress in the robes of Buddhist monks. When dressed simply in masculine attire, they can push their cause by putting on a white cotton face mask, as if they were suffering from a cold in the head, thus disguising a perhaps too-feminine mouth. Breasts are usually no trouble. Thus transmogrified, they can run the gamut of gay subterfuges among even the moodiest of men – especially, perhaps, those who usually enjoy women but who for some reason like lack of money, bad luck, loss of youthful charms or simply the desire to obey the beat of a different drum have a desire to infiltrate the gay community. It's mostly hand-holding, hip-squeezing, bottom-stroking, mutual masturbation – sometimes to the point of climax, which can be awkward unless one has a hanky ready. The better-mannered men always produce their own handkerchief or non-rustle tissue to wipe one dry after a satisfactory ejaculation. There is quite a lot of sucking going on, too, in the darker reaches. All these ploys are within a woman's range, if she goes about things in a perspicacious manner. But intercrural sex, which is also fairly common, would be a give-away. As for sodomy, the alert woman has to keep exploring fingers away from her genital region, and most gays do not appreciate one-way traffic. And should she be unmasked, everyone moves away from her, as if she were a pariah. Then the only thing for her to do is to eclipse herself into the light of day with as much good grace as possible.'

After this long speech Major Hilary Sitfast was visibly aroused, his modest bump showing clearly under his thigh-hugging jeans. Hideki gave an hysterical hoot at the sight and covered 'her' mouth with coy fingers, then continued the saga.

'But on the whole, Rolerei, I would not recommend visiting such places if one is a woman of the West. For example, your breasts would require tight binding, which would be unpleasant, as these dens of iniquity are usually overheated, in more senses than one. You would have to wear a black wig or a tight black head covering of some kind, like a ski-cap or a

Balaclava helmet, and something to hide your eyes – a pair of very big and very dark sun-glasses, which would look odd in a cinema. Besides, in Japan, they are often the trade mark of a gangster or *yakuza* or petty hoodlums, often sexually immature, called *chinpira* – which you should not confuse with *chinpo*, common parlance for prick, door-knocker, dick, bald-headed hermit or frigamajig.'

'Or giggle-stick, gravy-maker, holy poker, life-preserver, merrymaker, one-eyed milkman, plugtail, rump-splitter, spike-faggot, tally-whacker, tug-mutton, weapon, whacker, yard and ying-yang,' the Major perorated with accomplished euphemistic fluency.

'And balls are *kintama* or "eggs of gold",' Lorelei recapped.

'Or mountain oysters . . .'

'Or seed packets . . .'

'Or Beecham's pills . . .'

'Clangers, clappers, clockweights . . .'

'Cobblers' awls and coffee stalls . . .'

'The family diamonds . . .'

'The marbles, the knackers, the nutmegs . . .'

'The swingers, testimonials and twiddle-diddles . . .'

They might have gone on for ever exchanging saucy synonyms, when Hilary suddenly caught sight of Kenji 'call me Ken', his last night's lay. The Major turned pale. 'Quick!' he commanded his companions. 'We've got to get out of here before I'm spotted. . . .'

And they all took to their heels, to a well-concealed public convenience.

✺ 13 : Having a Tinkle

✺ Kenji had seen the Major and his companions disappearing into the comparative anonymity of the public toilets. He observed that only the one in a kimono seemed a bit confused about whether to enter the 'Men' or the 'Women' section. (Most of the public toilets in Japan are unisex, used by males and females.) Kenji decided not to pursue the matter any further: there were three against one. The Major had refused to pay him what he had demanded the night before. But he would get his own back. He had his ways of putting pressure on delinquent foreigners. One of his lovers was high up in the secret police. . . .

Lorelei found her cubicle in the toilet very disappointing. There were no holes in the solidly constructed walls, no spaces at the bottom under which exploring hands could be slipped, no graffiti. She had entered the one cubicle marked *Western Style*. It was spotlessly clean – rather dispiritingly so, quite asexual in fact. She decided that, as they were likely to be in hiding for a while, she might as well take advantage of the occasion and have a tinkle.

'Take a whizz, do a rural, drain the radiator, point Percy at the porcelain, train Terence on the terracotta. . . .'

Lorelei mused over some of the piss-provoking poeticisms as she copiously let fly: too much coffee.

Just as she was sprinkling the salad, there came a furtive knock at her door. The only word Lorelei felt familiar with in Japanese was *sayonara*, so she kept silent. 'Anyone in?' squeaked a little voice in immaculate Janglish. Lorelei held her breath, then knocked back without answering. Whoever it was shuffled on and found a vacant cubicle, from which came a loud rustling of papers and the slam of a suitcase lid. It was one of the schoolgirls changing out of her gym-dress into some fantasticated outfit. Lorelei stood on the seat and peeped over the partition – yes, the girl was next door, stark naked, only about fourteen, and masturbating with one of those painted wooden folk-art dolls with the phallic shanks, known as *kokeshi*.

'Do you need any help?' Lorelei inquired sweetly. 'You might do yourself an injury with that devilish dildo.'

Startled, the girl looked up and screamed 'Wah!' in dismay at the sight of a foreign face, a blue-eyed blonde devil. There was a hasty fumbling and scampering as Lorelei subsided in disappointment on the toilet seat, then the next door banged and she heard the girl trotting out into the bushes to complete her change of costume, if not her sexual gratification.

Lorelei sighed. Not even the girls were willing. . . .

There came another knock. It was Hideki, alias Fumiko the geisha. No luck there either, Lorelei was sure.

'It's all clear now,' Hideki whispered. 'And the Major had a stroke of luck,' he added, as they left the Ladies.

'Stroke is the right word,' murmured the Major, zipping himself up tenderly, as he gazed after the retreating figure of a high-school boy in blue jeans, wooden sandals and uniform jacket, from whose loose celluloid collar the neck of a pink polo-shirt peeped.

'What a mixture of styles!' remarked Lorelei.

'Yes. It's usually those mixed-up kids who are most ready and willing,' glowed the Major. 'But it's most unusual. Japan is not a land, generally speaking, for tea-room trade. Though there is one place in Nagoya Station . . .'

'For those who like old men,' Hideki sniffed contemptuously.

'If you can't get a woman, get a clean old man,' warbled Hilary – a song from his army days, when he had been a mere second lieutenant.

They spent the rest of the evening fairly conventionally in the upper circle of the Kabukiza, where they enjoyed the expert comments of Hideki on the talents of the female impersonators known as *onnagata*. 'You wouldn't believe some of the things they get up to when out in drag! And the old ones are as bad, if not as successful, as the young sprigs.'

'First classes tomorrow!' groaned Lorelei as they parted at her door. When, oh when would she obtain satisfaction? What was the matter with these Japanese men?

☀14 : The Cambridge English Academy

☀Major Hilary Sitfast called for Lorelei, as promised, at seven-thirty on Monday morning. Her first class at his Yoyogi cram school was due to start at nine. She had asked Hilary what she ought to wear.

'Something nunlike, I suggest, darling,' the Major had advised her. 'These modern boys take a lot of arousing. They've been emasculated by smothering mothers – "education mamas" as they are called – and by long hours of cramming useless knowledge and frivolous facts into their empty noddles. Nevertheless, I should not appear too *décolletée*. There are usually one or two brutal sadists in each class, and bullying is a terrible problem. We don't want you to be attacked on your first day, do we? A suit of solemn black, maybe. At most, iridescent cavalry twill.'

Lorelei was not so sure. She was by now in such a state of sexual tension, she would have welcomed a little rough treatment, as long as it came from something in trousers – or rather, something *not* in trousers.

She compromised by putting on the all-black costume of tights and long velvet jerkin she had acted in during the very short run of the first all-women production of *Hamlet*. The first line of her celebrated soliloquy had been rewritten to run: 'Is she, or isn't she? That is the question. . . .' It had been easy enough to cast the Queen, in the person of a famous female impersonator, and Ophelia, rising androgynous pop star, a madly smiling youth with pretty plucked eyebrows, spiky green-and-white hair, and the air of a wildly attractive schoolgirl who has just discovered she has a 'pash' on the maths mistress.

'The jerkin is no shorter than the average miniskirt,' she mused, admiring herself in a full-length mirror that went with

the apartment, though in order to save space it had been affixed
to the ceiling – a position that might serve other ends, thought
Lorelei dreamily, as she lay flat on her back admiring her legs.
They were sheathed in the new Cool Cobweb tights with the
interesting pseudo-ladder effects provocatively emphasizing
the calves and the succulent knee-pits which in Lorelei looked
so warm and vulnerable. She sat up and adjusted the swing of
her diamond chandelier earrings, which she was hoping would
become her trade mark ('symbol mark' was the Janglish term)
when she started her eventual modelling and T V career. She
wondered if she should fasten on her gilt feetcuffs, which she
hoped to mass-produce and publicize as 'The Vain Chain',
with sly references to 'Chain Reaction' in commercials. She
decided against them: they were a mite troublesome whenever
she had to part her thighs in a hurry. However, as a tribute
to the good old British public-school tradition, she donned
a sumptuous Eton collar of industrial diamonds, with fake
sapphires scattered here and there in lieu of ink-stains. Very
appropriate for one's first day at school. She wondered if there
would be any violent ragging, or any masochistic fagging.

The Major arrived in a pearl-grey three-piece suit, white
shirt and the tie of some decently obscure regiment: he didn't
want any awkward questions if he should meet the genuine
article. Only a *plain* monocle, on a simple black moiré silk
ribbon – 'It terrifies the shit out of new boys.'

He swept into Lorelei's apartment borne on a cloud of his
personal scent, Man Fan, and of the new after-shave lotion,
Milord, which the makers claimed was 'something more than
just another after-shave lotion – it takes courage to apply it –
prove your manhood this very morning by sloshing it all over
your body – it takes the wrinkles out of your scrotum better
than Helena Rubinstein's anti-wrinkle cream!' The Major had
penned the advertising copy with his own fair hand.

The Major looked archly at her Hamlet get-up. 'Well, at
least it's *black*,' he commented. 'And with black you can't go
wrong.'

'Oh, can't you?' throbbed Lorelei Thrillingly. 'Black can
look so *fast*, especially when it's well cut, as someone in darling
Ronald Firbank once pointed out.'

'It's the rush-hour, dear, so I hope you've got your tin pants on. At this hour the subway's as delirious as the Kabutocho in a panic.'

'What's that? The Stock Exchange trying cheque-book diplomacy.'

They sauntered to the station in perfectly blinding April morning sunshine which at once depressed them both.

'I find bright sunshine so lowering,' moaned Lorelei, putting on an outsize pair of graduated sun-glasses.

'Me too,' agreed Major Sitfast, adjusting his own amber-framed, amber-chained black goggles, which gave him a ghostly, gangster look.

The train was jam-packed. All along the platform virile young students doing part-time railway work were shoving the bottoms of passengers (and even other parts), packing them ever more tightly into the already crammed carriages so that the automatic doors could close. It was stifling. Hilary took care to have himself crushed up against one of the Self-Defence Force cadets on their way to Headquarters at Ichigaya. He was a well-built, stolid young professional soldier, and he did not blink an eyelash when he felt his well-hung equipment rising and stiffening in response to someone's questing fingers. Well, thought the Major, if *that's* what they call 'Self Defence', it'll be a walk-over for the Russians when they arrive.

Lorelei was less fortunate. She was pressed up against a Christian missionary whose hands were occupied with an office boy's bottom, while behind her an obvious woman-hater was protecting his private parts from the revolting softness of her bum by interposing a hard, cold metal attaché case. Fortunately, for Lorelei at any rate, the trip to Yoyogi did not take very long. The Major was wishing it could have endured for ever. But just as they had had to be pummelled on to the train, now they had to be hauled out, so tightly were they all stuck together, by more brawny young part-timers, one of whom managed to get his hand up Lorelei's jerkin, all the time keeping a totally blank expression on his simian face as he yanked her out and turned his attention to a girl secretary with breasts like teacups.

'It's like this every morning,' Hilary warned her, with an

ecstatic smile. 'And in the evenings too, of course, what they call "the U-turn". But the boys seem more sexy early in the morning.'

* * *

The Cambridge English Academy for Business English was situated in a back street on the fifth floor of a grimy, dilapidated office building. There was no lift, and by the time they got to the fifth floor Major Sitfast and Lorelei were panting and perspiring. It was a very humid day. The sun in the streets had seemed like liquid heat.

'Here is the staff-room,' the Major said, making the familiar Japanese bow and 'ushering' gesture as she preceded him into a tiny, dark cupboard of a room with a small, low table and one armchair covered with a dubious white *housse*. A metal Johnny Walker tray and some glasses by Suntory stood on the table, together with equipment for making green tea – five unmatched, handleless cups and a teapot with a disintegrating woven bamboo handle and a cracked lid. Cutlery courtesy Korean Air.

'Take a shit – I mean *seat*,' laughed Hilary. 'How soon one falls into these little traps of pronunciation when one hears them all day long!'

Lorelei lowered her seductive bottom gingerly into the armchair, which felt as if it was made of stone. When she complained about it, the Major explained: 'That's typical Japanese upholstery, love. They've been using chairs only for the last hundred years or so, and they still haven't discovered how to make them. You might be more comfortable sitting on the floor.'

Lorelei looked down in distaste at the moth-eaten moquette and stayed where she was.

'I'm afraid you have to share the toilet with us men,' simpered the Major. 'It's the usual Japanese unisex arrangement, and it's a squatter, just a hole in the floor, but it does flush. It's not one of those places still so common in Japan where the turds and whey have to be syphoned off every week or so by the honey-cart.'

'Did you say "us men"?' Lorelei demanded, her interest quickening.

'Well, in a manner of speaking.'

This was explained by the whirlwind entry of the Major's 'private secretary for internal affairs', Sadaharu.

'Call me "Sad" or "Rue",' he lisped as they were introduced after the Major had planted an airy kiss on his high cheekbones.

Sad was plying a small fan of bitter orange silk liberally spangled with blue diamonds and Je Reviens (the pirated Taiwanese substitute), a small flagon of which dangled on a platinum chain from the red-stitched buttonhole of his lilac cashmere casual suit. 'I make tea, clean table, dust pictures,' he said, pointing to coloured reproductions of the Queen and her Consort, and another of Prince Charles and Diana, Princess of Wales. They all looked distinctly miffed to be seen there.

Sad (or was it Rue?) pointed to the picture of Charles and Diana, and informed Lorelei in his almost immaculate American-accented English: 'We Japanese like him. He young, have funny face, like monkey.'

'And what about Princess Diana?' Lorelei asked.

'We Japanese like her. She young, have funny face, like English rose.'

'I could hardly agree much more,' she replied, languishing at him, and giving the phrase that subtle rhythm of 'heightened speech' she had learnt during a week's engagement at Margate in *The Elder Statesman*, which had bored the old-age pensioners silly. Eliot trying to crack a joke was as much of a flop as Samuel Beckett on ice. *Waiting for Godot* is an awfully long skate.

'Please again, more slowly?'

Sad was a personable young thing, more intelligent even than he looked, but he had been brought up on the rather blunt standards of American culture, and 'the Queen's English' often baffled the dear boy. He was wearing one of the new tangerine wigs, in the 'chrysanthemum cut', cunningly flecked here and there with silver, to give an air of interesting experience. The doll, he was only just turned eighteen, and the idol of all the American bases.

'We Japanese not understand Queen's English,' he tittered, hiding his perfect lips and teeth with his fan, over the top of which he looked roguishly at the Major, in a pose he had learnt from innumerable movies on the theme of *Carmen*. In order to make agreeable conversation with this probably quite unimportant personage (but one never knew, did one?), Lorelei passed flattering comments on Sad's long, artificial fingernails, of a pearly black plastic substance that contrasted vividly with the hairless magnolia pallor of his slender, limp, waxen hands, with moons of an almost futuristic white.

'Say, thanks,' he smiled, bowing. Then, surprisingly: 'And what are your politics, Miss Thrillingly?'

'I'm liberal, in every sense of the word.'

'We Japanese not understand politics. We Japanese liberal also, but better, Liberal Democratic, yes.' He pointed to a large photograph of the entire Liberal Democratic Cabinet posing in a stiff samurai group, wearing baggy striped trousers and ill-fitting black tailcoats, outside the Prime Minister's residence.

As she gazed at those very plain elderly men, Lorelei could not help thinking of all those dreary dongs dangling inside their pants.

'Prime Minister have hair-style we Japanese call *sudare* – like matchstick blinds,' explained Sad, pointing to the Prime Minister's carefully combed remnants of hair stretched across his blank skull. They did indeed look like those exotic tropical shadows cast by blinds in Somerset Maugham or Tennessee Williams movies.

'They look more like a bar code,' suggested Hilary.

Loud yells and shrieks were coming from the corridor outside.

'The boys are arriving,' explained the Major. 'In a few moments I'll conduct you to your classroom and introduce you.'

'We Japanese very noisy,' tittered Sad. 'I make you nice cup of green tea after your class.'

The Major accompanied Lorelei to a large classroom occupied by about a hundred students, mostly boys. An unnatural hush fell over them as they entered and took up positions in front of a green board on which was chalked *Wercome to Camblidge Engrish Acodomy Rady Rolerei!!!* Lorelei wondered if it was meant to rhyme with 'sodomy'.

'Good morning, everyone,' the Major enunciated slowly, very brightly.

The response came just as slowly, and very sluggishly: 'Good morning, Major Hiraly Shitfast.'

'This is your new teacher from England, Miss Lorelei Thrillingly.'

The students, who had collapsed into subdued giggles after greeting the Major in English, now gave way to greater mirth. The girls held their hands over their mouths, and some of the boys did too, while others laid their arms on their desks and buried their heads in them, their shoulders shaking.

'Don't worry, dear. It's just embarrassment. The usual reaction when they have to say a few words of English. I'll leave you to them. All you have to do is chatter away and ask a few questions if you like, but I can guarantee you'll get no answers. *Bon courage!*'

'Well,' Lorelei began with her brightest smile. 'What shall we talk about this morning?'

No answer. The students all sat up, deadly serious, and gazed at her in stunned incomprehension. Lorelei waited patiently for suggestions. After a few moments one of the male students was viciously prodded by his neighbours and made to stand up. He was going to make a speech!

'I will come to poke you!' is what Lorelei thought she heard.

'Please do!' she countered vivaciously. 'But wait till after the class.'

The boy sat down, covered in blushes and confusion, amid universal giggles. Lorelei realized they could not understand a word she said. And to her disappointment she also realized that the boy had said 'Welcome to Tokyo'. She sighed, but with a smile, remembering an old Chinese proverb: 'If you don't have a smiling face, don't open a shop.' The same maxim might be applied, she felt, to teaching English as a Foreign Language.

'Welcome to Tokyo' seemed to be the only words the boy knew. Lorelei wondered what it would be like in bed with him – he was quite a burly young thug type. Would he pant in the midst of orgasm 'Welcome to Tokyo, Miss Thrillingly?' She would have to teach him some new words. O to become a 'sleeping dictionary'! 'What is your name?' she asked a boy who

was the only one in the front row. All the others had taken seats
as far to the back of the class as possible.

The boy giggled helplessly at her, scratched his head and
turned round to ask the others, in Japanese, some urgent
question. The whole class started tittering. Then the boy turned
back to Lorelei, and said: 'I am a boy.'

'Well yes, I can see that.' Lorelei smiled graciously. 'But
what is your name?'

'I do not know – it!' the boy brought out triumphantly,
collapsing with the rest of the class into hysterical laughter.

'I cannot believe a grown boy like you would not know his
own name,' Lorelei said teasingly. 'Come on, now, tell me who
you are.'

There were further long discussions with the rest of the class,
all in Japanese, of course. Lorelei noticed that when they spoke
in Japanese, their voices were loud and confident. But when
they managed a few words of English, they spoke almost in
whispers, as if terrified of making a mistake.

Lorelei turned to one of the girls. She had a plump, pasty
face and long, lank black hair which she kept tossing about
from one side to the other, sometimes half blinding the boys
behind her. Or she would pick up strands and twist them in her
grubby fingers in a manner Lorelei found decidedly unappeal-
ing, though the girl obviously thought she was being 'cute'.

'What is your name?' Lorelei asked her.

The girl stopped playing with her hair and gaped at Lorelei
in a state of shock, then sprawled over her desk in a fit of
uncontrollable hilarity.

'She is a pen,' said somebody.

'I am a pen,' the girl spluttered, then had hysterics again.

Lorelei gave up that 'direct' approach. 'I'll sing you a song,'
she told them. 'An English song.'

'Please sing song.'

'We Japanese like sing song.'

So, with a sigh, Lorelei started belting out:

> 'If you want coffee,
> Go to Brazil,
> And go to Spain

For the matador's kill,
But if you want a man –
Go to Japan.
You can't fail –
It's the Tokyo Tale.'

They clapped politely, but the song was apparently not to their liking. One young man at the back of the class asked Lorelei to sing 'Homo Sweet Homo', a song with which she was unfamiliar.

'We Japanese love "Homo Sweet Homo".'

'Or "Rock Romond".'

Fortunately, at that moment some tinny chimes rang out – imitation Big Ben chimes! Lorelei felt a trifle nostalgic. But the sound was so cheap and harsh, she felt more indignant than sad. She was to discover that the whole of Japan is submerged all day long under these deadly electronic chimes, from busy city streets to the remotest mountain village schools. They are everywhere. They even disturb the peace of Zen monasteries and divide the long days of prisons and lunatic asylums. 'Bing-Bong-Bing-Bang! Bang-Bing-Bing-Bong. . . .' It was a senseless sound, one of the many useless noises of Japan that were to haunt her dreams. But now her first lesson was over.

'Goodbye everyone,' she called out, waving brightly as she made for the door.

'Goot-o-bai!' one daring girl replied, and the whole class subsided once more into uncontrollable laughter.

Lorelei felt as if she had been hit over the head with rubber hammers. Her jaws ached with smiling. She had been gritting her teeth so hard, they might well have been ground to powder. As she tottered into the staff-room, Sad poured her a cup of green tea. She sank on to the megalithic armchair.

'You like quick shot of something zippy?'

She barely had the strength to nod and Sad poured a stiff dose of tequila ('by the makers of Nikka whisky') into her tea.

'Where's Major Sitfast?' she managed to gasp after the first mouthful.

'He on important business,' Sad simpered. 'Give his students day off. Very kind. Always vacation time here.'

Lorelei took the hint. Faced by the stony silence, then the uncontrollable giggles of her next class, 'Office Conversation', she gave up the unequal struggle and simply recited:

> 'There were three ravens sat in a tree,
> They were as black as black might be. . . .'

The whole class echoed her in a slow, drone-like reactivated sludge:

> 'There were thlee lavens shat in a tlee,
> They were as brack as brack might be. . . .'

Everyone was obviously very relieved when she stopped the class well before time. The students all rushed off to have driving lessons or tennis coaching, subjects infinitely more important than mere Business English.

The Major was back in the staff-room when she arrived. 'That's right, dear,' he said, glancing at his Mickey Mouse wrist-watch. 'Just send them packing if you don't feel up to it.'

'I feel like a limp rag,' moaned Lorelei.

'I know the feeling,' sympathized the Major. 'It's a feeling we all get after two minutes of conversation with most Japanese.'

Lorelei took another shot of green tea and tequila from Sad's ministering hands. The sight of his hands made her feel quite queasy.

'But I already have such good reports of you,' the Major went on brightly. 'The students like you. They're very dress-conscious, and your unique style appeals to their sense of humour.'

'I couldn't stop them giggling,' complained Lorelei.

'That's just embarrassment at having to say a few words of English in front of the rest of the class. They think English is the world's biggest joke. But you're looking rather peaky, sweet one. Take the rest of the day off. I'll give the whole school a holiday to celebrate your arrival.'

'Thank Buddha,' sighed Lorelei. She felt that if she had to face another class, she would just wither away.

'I've got some business to see to, Sad, so do see the premises are locked up.'

'Yes, Major sir. I think I go to Kabutocho see how my money game is doing. Lucky boys working there. . . . Such a crush on the Stock Exchange floor.'

The Major laughed a pearly laugh. 'Yes, all those fresh young men in sober pants, satin-backed waistcoats and virginal shirt-sleeves like mixing business with pleasure. They keep feeling each other up as they shout the exchange rates. The Japanese like nothing better than being in a permanent crush.'

'Yes,' said Sad. 'I watch from Visitors' Gallery. I quite blue with envy.'

'Tomorrow, dear,' the Major said, turning back to Lorelei, 'you need not arrive dead on time as we did today. Take half an hour off at the end, too. They like to be kept waiting.'

'As dear Sir Donald Wolfit used to say when taking his curtain calls: "Let them know you're coming." So perhaps Sad could keep popping in to let them know of my progress from time to time . . .'

'She leave her apartment . . . she walking down Ginza to subway . . . she get no seat on subway . . . she meet nice young *yakuza* in white suit . . . he feel her bottom . . . she going up escarator . . . she turn corner . . . she bump into handsome young karate instluctor . . . he aporridgize . . . she smile, she say "my pressure" . . . she velly happy . . . she coming up stairs . . . she powering her rittle nose . . . she lunning arong collidor . . . she here! At which point the class bursts into generous applause,' said the Major. 'And I advise you to wear a new outfit every day. They have chronically short attention spans, these new-age kids. They want something new to get their attention every day.'

'Then I'll be needing a clothes allowance!'

'I'm afraid we can't run to that, darling. Now I must rush. I have some important business.'

I wonder what his mysterious business is? thought Lorelei. And how am I to pay for a new outfit every day?

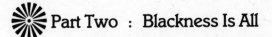 Part Two : Blackness Is All

Too black for heav'n, and yet too white for hell.
John Dryden, *The Hind and the Panther*

✳15 : The Black and Black Bar

✳Sir Paul Pinker, the British Cultural Society's representative poof, had discovered one of the rare, last B Y O G (Bring Your Own Glass) homo bars in the wilds of Shibuya. He was what they call in Japan a 'veteran', not on account of his late middle age but because he was a regular – that is, he had been there at least more than once.

It was a gloomy sort of place, with padded black leather walls and a black formica counter decorated with funerary lanterns from a nearby Buddhist funeral director's that had gone bankrupt. People no longer trusted the money-grubbing Zen priests and their curious sexual practices that had got confused with the burial and cremation rites. So they were joining in droves the new religions that offered to dispose of one's ashes in space at a reduced rate, via the Prince Genji Jet Propulsion Laboratory's space shuttle, *Sexy*.

There was a peculiarly pungent smell coming from the basement toilet, and all the drinks seemed to taste of it – a mixture of methylated spirits, air freshener of an unknown floral variety, and low-grade embalming fluid. Sir Paul was allowed the veteran's privilege of mixing his own drinks. For his Blue Gins, he used the 'house bottle' which was kept for him under the sink, and his Mount Fuji fountain-pen, loaded with fresh Waterman's every evening. And he carried a collapsible metal cup from his poofy Boy Scout days.

He generally went there after a late dinner, round about ten o'clock, when things were a little livelier and some of the mortuary stink had been blanketed in cheap local cigarette-smoke touted by the Government tobacco monopoly with the slogan *Nice Day, Nice Choking*. A more inscrutable one ran *We are the Smokes!* It was typical of the new kind of bars where regular

95

customers kept their own bottles of liquor, labelled with their names – a 'Bottle Keep'.

The music was lugubrious, repetitive, monotonous, ear-blasting hard rock, to which the customers did some old-fashioned cheek-to-cheek, pelvis-to-pelvis jog-trot dancing.

Here Sir P was wont to meet members of the foreign diplomatic and artistic set to discuss palpitating issues like the amateur productions of *The Mousetrap* by TTT (Top Tokyo Thespians) or of *Smilin' Thru'* by the Kinki Kyoto Kids. But their chief purpose was to pick up boys. They called it 'seeking recruits for the Orphan Children of Traffic Accidents Extraordinary'. These country boys from remote provincial towns and villages were runaways from their stifling rural homes who saw no future in planting rice and raising a family in some bigoted, gossip-ridden, superstitious, boring Government-sponsored community. The Tokyo police managed to catch a fair number of them when they landed from the north at Ueno Station. But Sir Paul and his set had their own talent-spotters there, some of them discreetly bribed members of the police. And there were those passionate boys, hot as Latins, and coming from the southern islands where the samurai honour tradition of manly love still flourished, who kept arriving at Osaka, Kyoto, Nagoya and Tokyo Stations, desperate for a night's lodging. Sir Paul had his contacts all over the archipelago. 'Bring him to the Orphanage' was his reaction when someone telephoned news of a particularly luscious specimen from Kagoshima or Kumamoto.

One night at the Black and Black Bar (as it was called, in imitation of a TV toothpaste commercial for White and White dentifrice) Sir P sat watching the TV set. The programmes were as usual boring as hell – mostly baseball and Diet deliberations interspersed with crude commercials couched in a curious mixture of debased Japanese and even more debased English. There were innumerable inane quizzes, and there was the non-singing of hundreds of no-talent 'idols' – teenage morons with little-girl affectations and infantile one-note songs. But just occasionally a nice-looking boy would prance across the screen, showing a bit of bottom. They never showed the least sign of a 'bump' at the front, not because they did not have sexual equipment of a miniature variety, but because it was forbidden by law for any mature male performer to exhibit any signs of sexual arousal – or even repose – in public. It was all part of the paradox of life in Japan, where porno mags were available from slot-machines at every street corner, yet the outward demeanour of the general public was prim and proper, even prudish, and where anything that was 'deleterious to public morals' was officially banned but continued to flourish in accepted environments like saunas, movies, peeping Tom parks, no-panty coffee shops, houses of assignation or 'love hotels' and an infinite number of cabarets and bars. Yet the majority of Japanese men had the air of being permanently sexually frustrated. They had the hangdog look of the overhung. No wonder they worked off their inhibitions in subways and cinemas and strip shows. Some men were so desperate for sex that at 'live shows' they had no hesitation in getting up on the stage, stripping and performing sex acts with men and woman and animals.

'It's a never-never society where anything goes,' mused Sir Paul as he sipped his third Blue Gin and stroked the warm, black velvet thighs of the youth on the next bar stool, who was taking no notice whatsoever of this approach, as his own fingers were on the flies of a Brazilian playboy on his other side.

Sir Paul observed that new British girl, Lorelei Thrillingly, prancing across the screen in an ad for sanitary napkins, showing a good deal of crutch and a very protruberant vulva – it was all right for women to show themselves off like that. Sir P felt unusually disgruntled. That idiotic Lorelei, whom Sitfast had brought out as an English conversation teacher, had made great progress in other fields during the past year. The British Cultural Society liked to keep a firm control on education and culture in Japan, allowing only its own chosen darlings, veritable incompetents, to operate under the British flag. Lorelei and the Major had escaped their net, and so were to be discouraged at every turn. But Lorelei and the Major were not so easily kept down. She was on cosmetics posters all over town, snuggling half-naked in the arms of some butch, dyke-looking pseudo-geisha. It was really incredible, the amount of lesbian imagery today in Japanese advertising – all part of the

universal spread of peeping Tomism. Then she had had a huge
success as Lady Macbeth in an all-nude movie production of
Macbeth by that idiot director Oshima. That had definitely *not*
had the support of the BCS, and Sir Paul had received a
frightful wigging from the London office for not suppressing
it by hook or by crook.

As for the Major, he was forever on the up and up, promoting
Lorelei and writing barbed criticisms of Japanese society in the
local papers, mostly attacking right-wing nationalists and the
cult of the war dead at the Yasukuni Shrine – a dangerous
undertaking these days.

'Give him enough rope and he'll hang himself' was Hunter
Elvet's sage advice to Sir Paul Pinker.

In self-defence, the Major would riposte: 'Someone must
trespass on the taboos of modern nationalism, in the interests
of human reason. Business can't. Diplomacy won't. It has to
be people like us.'

He did not reveal that he had extracted these telling
phrases from an out-of-print travel book on Russia by his
old friend Robert Byron, alas long since dead and gone. . . .
But fortunately for the Major, his merry mask of a gay caballero
prevented all but the most percipient – of whom there were few
in Japan – from taking him seriously, and that suited him fine.

'But you and I have all the Japanese academics on our side,'
Sir P explained to Hunny. 'They know that we are in a position
to award them bursaries and travel grants for "study trips" of
a year and more in England or the USA. As these scholars
are no less opportunistic than Japanese businessmen, artists
and politicians, they will always accept our advice about what
foreigners to appoint to teaching posts – always our own people,
of course. The Major and his lot don't stand a chance. No
Japanese professor would dare to run counter to our orders
and appoint a non-BCS applicant, for fear of being blacklisted
and refused a bursary.'

But the continued successes of non-official *personae non gratae*
like the Major were both worrying and inexplicable. . . .

His broodings were interrupted by the entrance of Kenji,
a boy he had not met before but to whom Sir P at once felt
attracted. Kenji was 'his type' – good-natured to the point of

stupidity, and with a desirable young body under his black corduroys. He was showing a modest but promising bump, too.

But Kenji was not just a packet of gropable gonads. His blank clown's face and sexy dumbness were masks for a pretty sharp intelligence. The Major had soon found out his mistake in thinking Kenji was not 'switched on'. Since that night at the Russian coffee shop with Hideki, the Major had had some difficult moments with young Kenji, who kept asking for more money than the Major thought he was worth. Sir P was blissfully unaware of all this when he invited Kenji to sit beside him, and plied him with drinks as he stroked, with all the passion of an elderly erotomaniac, the velvety ribbed cloth of Kenji's shapely thighs and quickly bulging genital area. It was so very difficult to hold a conversation in the ear-splitting blasts from the hi-fi, so body language was an accepted means of communication at the Black and Black Bar.

Sir Paul was feeling especially horny, and in need of relaxation, as he had spent most of the past week finishing the writing of Taro's graduation thesis: 'Some Environmental Aspects Governing the Subtext of *Rebecca of Sunnybrook Farm*, with Special Reference to Certain Agronomic Imponderables'. He hadn't the faintest idea what it meant. But, as in everything in Japan, appearance was all, and a resoundingly abstract title was bound to attract top marks. Yet Taro had so far proved ungrateful: he kept worrying about the final exams, which were to be held next week. Sir P, through his academic contacts, had managed to get an advance look at the question papers, and passed the photocopies on to Ta-Ta. But the dear boy had said they were useless without the answers: Japanese professorial examiners expect examinees to reproduce exactly the official answers they have devised for each question. Any departure from the often illogical or even incorrect answers dreamt up by the standardized system of the teaching profession would be severely penalized. Even though Sir P had written a masterly title and an even more masterly abstraction of a thesis for him, Taro could easily fail to pass his finals.

Kenji had begun shyly massaging Sir Paul's rather loose genitals. At his age, they usually required more stimulation

than that to give him a reasonable cock-stand. But it was
a pleasurable sensation all the same, and helped Sir P to
bear a spate of domestic commercials for lavatory cleansers,
Mamma Royal washing-up liquid and an infinite variety of
cheap snacks in which the women were noticeably becoming
much more dominating, the husbands cowering under their
lashing tongues or being made to look foolish in front of their
tittering brats. Yes, women were taking over everywhere, there
was no escaping them, even in the monasteries of sacred Mount
Koyasan, from which they used to be excluded as unclean.
All the bars were packed every night with drunken teenage
girls, and the 'Apollo' bars were for 'Ladies Only'. Men were
not allowed to play with their own sex in such feminine
haunts, where bored housewives were serviced by students,
Self-Defence Forces recruits and police cadets working part-
time. High-school teachers and university professors were
complaining that after particularly heavy nights pandering
to the whims of oversexed housewives neglected by their
husbands, their better-looking students could hardly keep
their eyes open, were hung-over and fell asleep – though the
last was nothing new, given the atrocious boredom of most
teaching in Japan, where even after leaving school everyone
is still lectured to death.

'I come home with you,' Kenji was whispering, his strange,
young pale face quite blank.

Is he 'safe'? Sir Paul wondered.

As if reading his thoughts, Kenji added: 'I make no trouble.
I love you.'

Sir Paul had had enough experience of Japanese youth to
take.this with a large pinch of natural sea-salt. To the casual
observer from abroad, Japan seemed awash with love. Japanese
people never said they just 'liked' something, it was always
'loved', even if only a bar of chocolate or a new Toyota. The
repulsive heart symbol was everywhere – in banks, police
stations, ward offices, schools, businesses, on trains and buses
and ambulances. Slogans were everywhere, saying *I love my
Sony Walkman* or *I love My Home*, in which the word 'love'
had a crimson heart symbol substituted for it. The word
'love', and the human feeling normally associated with it,

had become completely atrophied and debased, as if people no longer knew or trusted the real emotion or were afraid of it. In the slogan *We love our Tokyo* the heart symbol was doubled, to express the plural. How inhuman can they get? wondered Sir Paul. So he exercised a natural caution when he asked Kenji: 'How much?'

'How much?' The blank face might have been expressing blank shock. On the other hand, it might have been expressing nothing.

'Yes,' replied Sir Paul firmly. 'How much?'

'I not business boy.'

'I did not say you were. I just asked how much you want.'

'All night, or short time?'

'It depends on you.'

'OK. What you like?'

'Everything you have to offer.'

'You got Aids? I got condoms.'

'No. Have *you* got Aids?'

'Japanese boys no have. I got condoms six different colours.'

'All right. Let's go.' Sir Paul paid the 'checks' and they left the bar.

As soon as they had left, the bartender picked up the black telephone and dialled a certain number.

✳ 16 : Laughter Unlimited

✳ Lorelei was beginning to like Japan. At first, it had been hell. She had hated teaching English conversation, and soon realized that was because she had no gift for teaching, and no training. The strange thing was that her students used to enjoy her lessons: they found her a perpetual source of wonder and entertainment. They seemed to be forever smiling and laughing – but laughing *with* her, not *at* her.

Indeed, she soon became aware of the force of laughter in Japanese life. Wherever she went, she felt herself surrounded by a sort of underground stream of all kinds of laughter, lapped by a constant rippling of giggles, titters, cascades of girlish glee, feminine frivolity and masculine mirth. It was as if, in order to offset the drabness and grimness of ordinary daily life, the Japanese had acquired the gift of laughter as a priceless decoration on the sober background of existence. All the masses of blackness in clothes, uniforms and hair were illuminated by this golden thread of levity, much of it quite capricious and meaningless. 'Three little maids from school are we' from *The Mikado* was no comic opera invention but one of the essential truths of feminine life. Everywhere pairs and groups of schoolgirls and women were laughing in the most abandoned way, giggling until tears came to their eyes, holding polite hands or spread fingers daintily over wide-open mouths and gold-flashing teeth in order to mask their incredible hilarity. Older women, housewives, would bend the forefinger of the right hand and lift it to the top lip, just under the nose, with the other fingers prettily curled, as a sign that they were amused by something and were trying in vain to restrain their ungovernable mirth. There was a Japanese saying that schoolgirls would laugh even if a pair of chopsticks fell on the

floor. Boys and men laughed at apparently the most simple
and innocent things, at the slightest accident or deviation from
the expected. To Lorelei, accustomed to the mainly unsmiling
societies of the West, such permanent merriment was both
a marvel and an irritation – it often seemed so infantile,
so mechanical. It was as if laughter were a living part of
the Japanese language, and that speech would no longer be
understood without its emollient, explanatory wordlessness.

Another source of interest for her, until it too became
annoyance, was the way groups of women would go for
a day's shopping as if they were little maids from school,
with high-pitched giggles, loud voices raised in endless gossip
and exchanges of useless information. Even women of forty
and fifty would act as if they were fifteen, and their girlish
affectations took on a grotesque cuteness when they dressed
in the latest little-girl fashions, their clothes covered with
artless embroideries and appliqué patterns, their handbags
and shopping bags ornamented with nursery rhyme or comic
cartoon figures. Often Lorelei felt she was the only grown-up
in a society of arrested adolescents.

So as soon as possible she gave up teaching, which exposed
her mercilessly to this unquenchable and tiresome artificial
joy all day long. She got jobs in shops and boutiques, in
department stores demonstrating how to put on make-up
or inviting customers to taste samples of sickly sweet 'corn
potage' or pizza cheese or slices of dark-green bread, the colour
obtained by mixing in green tea or spinach or seaweed with the
dough.

Soon she was doing modelling jobs for magazines and for the
avalanches of fliers shoved into letter-boxes and distributed on
the streets – opulent, shiny paper, beautifully coloured pictures
and photographs, all intended to entice the buyer; but each
sheet spelling the death of Japanese forests.

Magazine modelling led to fashion shows and to appear-
ances on TV to display the latest swim-wear, with the
cameras focused relentlessly on her crutch. She was the first
to introduce YSL's sequinned lycra swim-suits. She took part
in TV English language lessons, which never went above a
certain very elementary level. She had a good ear and soon

picked up 'survival Japanese', which admitted her to the ranks
of quiz programmes, in which there was generally a foreigner
to provide exotic interest and to bolster the ever-present
feelings of inferiority in the Japanese listeners through her
mistakes in pronunciation and grammar. There were many
such foreigners, who earned a good living acting as clowns and
jesters for a Japanese public avid for some kind of reassurance
that they were superior to Westerners. That was the price she
had to pay for having a bigger vulva, dramatically outlined in
her high-rise lycra swim-pants.

She eventually earned enough money to move out of her
dismal little apartment and into something brighter and more
spacious, though at what was an exorbitant rent. The Major
found it for her, and she suspected he shared some of the house
agent's huge commission. Hilary also got work for her, taking
a percentage of her earnings for acting as her agent. He was
still running his successful school, doing much of the teaching
himself, with the help of odd foreign drifters who would stay
for a few weeks, then move on to Bali or Katmandu or Sri
Lanka. Hideki, fluent in American English, often helped out
with teaching, passing himself off as a native Californian.
Sadaharu could not disguise his essential Japaneseness, but
was popular, especially with the women students who, like most
Japanese young girls, were fascinated by homosexual boys.

The Major had taken Lorelei to a 'normal' (that is, non-gay)
cinema to see homo movies like *Midnight Express*, *Cruising*, *A
Bigger Splash* and in particular *Another Country*, at which the
audiences were composed almost entirely of teenage girls.
When *Cruising* was shown, the girls were issued with maps of
the gay spots in Greenwich Village. Many of the girls were no
more than twelve or thirteen years old. The public schoolboys
in *Another Country* became their idols, though Lorelei thought
their 'best of Britain' good looks were rather too stereotyped
and conventional: she preferred something racier in a man,
something a bit off-centre, criminal, tough.

She had a hard time finding such men in Japan. Most of
them seemed to be either gay or suffering from severe mother
domination. The Major took her to Zen monasteries where the
young, sexually deprived monks were reputed to seize every

opportunity they could for passing sex. But the harsh life, the endless kneeling and bowing, the services beginning at three-thirty in the morning even on the harshest winter day, soon broke their spirit – and hers.

She had hoped the summer would bring her satisfaction, but the beaches and mountains were as crowded as the Ginza with androgynous youths whose only reaction to her near-nudity was to gape at her crutch, which had a generous bulge, and shout 'Harrow'. For a while she worked at Disneyland, outside the city, where there were several foreigners as guides and restaurant staff. But even they seemed to have become infected with the crudity and childishness of the place. For a while she performed as Snow White, walking in parades with Mickey Mouse and Donald Duck and all the other plastic stars of the Disney pantheon, but this seemed to set her even further apart from Japanese men, who when they came to Disneyland did so as fathers of families, acting like little boys out of school.

Summertime had been abnormally hot and humid. The only cool places were the pachinko parlours, where she would sit for hours playing the machines, occasionally accumulating enough ball-bearings to enable her to exchange them for tinned goods at the nearby trading shop. The men and women playing pachinko were like automatons, their gaze fixed permanently on the spinning balls as if they were drugged by the noise and the ear-splitting martial music which was dinned constantly into their unreceptive ears. They were like living vegetables.

Occasionally, at bookstores, record shops and art supply dealers, she would see attractive boys and men browsing. The Major had told her these were good places to pick up adolescents. But as soon as she approached them, they would look scared and run away. The closest she got was in bookstores, where youths intent on pornographic comics or magazines would be so absorbed in erotica that they did not realize they were displaying incipient erections, which Lorelei was sometimes able to encourage by brushing her hands against them as she pretended to pick up books from the low counters. But this ploy never brought her any true satisfaction. She felt eternally frustrated.

'The trouble is,' Major Sitfast explained, 'the Japanese now are so very self-conscious, through endless foreign criticism. So when they see a foreigner, they tend to avoid him or her, as they feel anything foreign means bother or trouble.'

The Major took her to a performance of the Takarazuka Girls' Troupe when it visited Tokyo from its home base near Kobe. The audience was filled with screaming adolescent girls in the throes of sentimental passion for their beloved stars, girls acting women's dramatic and singing roles in terribly feminine, old-fashioned style, while the *jeune premier* parts were played by mannish young women with artificially gruff voices and fake manly stance and walk. To Lorelei, it was all highly comical and frightfully kitsch. The girls on stage looked as if they had stepped out of the light operas of the last century, and their exaggerated make-up gave them the appearance of those coy and simpering young lovers on French twenties postcards. She met some of them in a lesbian bar named Yourcenar. But although she had enjoyed a number of lesbian affairs in Britain, these false creatures simply did not appeal at all to her rather special tastes.

So in the end, she gave up looking for a man, or for a woman, and concentrated on work and on earning as much money as possible, which she very wisely put into the bank and into investments.

Then Major Hilary Sitfast came with a proposition: he wanted her to seduce a certain young man.

'A Japanese?'

'Well yes, darling. I'm afraid so.'

Lorelei groaned.

'But he's awfully choice, dear. Something very special.'

'In what way?'

'You'll see. And there's a packet of money in it. . . .'

It was now late autumn. The weather was still fine and sunny, with just a slight crispness in the air in the early morning. But soon, Lorelei had been warned, would begin the preparations for the horrible Japanese Christmas, and – for a foreigner – the boredom and loneliness of the long New Year holidays. She would need a bit of excitement in her life if she were to survive the traditional New Year. So . . . it just might be good for a laugh.

✳17 : Drums of Departure

✳Hideki, alias Fumiko, the male geisha, was giving a party. It was to celebrate his new job. He/she was going on a long foreign tour to Europe and the United States. Hideki/Fumiko, so cute, so pretty, so much more feminine than any woman, had been engaged to join a company of drummers from the island of Hokkaido. The drummers were lusty young men who appeared on stage clad only in the tightest of breech-clouts and a virginal white towel rolled and knotted round their close-cropped heads, like the fillet of the Ancient Greek athletes. They looked tremendously virile, and their magnificent drumming on a wide variety of drums, some of them colossal, required real stamina and muscle. The sounds they produced, from the faintest whispers to the most thunderous hurricanes, from throbbing heartbeats to sophisticated rhythms of clicks produced by hitting the wooden rims of the drums with the drumsticks, were overwhelming in their precision and intensity. They were becoming the idols of every foreign homosexual community and, it was said, were not averse to a well-paid roll in the hay with both women and men. And after their long and sweaty performances, their unwashed breech-clouts or *fundoshi*, which so intimately clung to the cleft of those sinewy buttocks and lovingly fondled the cock and balls, fetched very inflated prices from the stage-door Johnnies, who regarded them as amulets against impotence, Aids or the clap.

Hideki had been engaged to 'soften' certain moments in the performance by music and dance in a more feminine mode, to provide contrast with the energetic macho-male numbers that formed the greater part of the programme. Because of his fluent English, he was also the troupe's interpreter – for of course such handsome hunks of sexy masculinity had never bothered to study languages. With their gorgeous bodies, words in any language were unnecessary. Hideki as Fumiko the male geisha would do one number in each half of the show, and link the acts with an English narrative lovingly composed by Major Hilary Sitfast, who had enjoyed doing research on the troupe at their all-male training quarters in the far north of the Hokkaido pine forests, where the first snows had already fallen.

'Sheer bliss!' was how he described his experiences to Lorelei, who cast an appreciative eye over the small group of leading drummers at the party. 'It's the breech-clouts that do it. So terribly exciting!'

'I can imagine,' moaned Lorelei, drinking in the indifferent male beauty of a sixteen-year-old star of the show. But he was too busy eating and drinking to notice anyone.

The drummers were not dressed in stage costume but in Western clothes, cut in Savile Row, London, where they had enjoyed a sensational triumph. The party was being held in a luxury hotel in Akasaka, a high-toned geisha and entertainment district. People kept getting up on the platform and bellowing folk-songs and pop songs and sentimental ballads called *enka* – a sort of Japanese Country and Western – to the backing of *karaoke* tapes, which provide the musical accompaniment without the voice. That has to be provided by the performer. And most of the performers were drunk and incapable, or simply had no musical sense. No one was listening anyhow. As at any Japanese party, all people wanted was to have a free feed and lots of free drinks. Elegance and conversation flew out of the window in the face of unbridled greed.

But Hideki/Fumiko remained his/her cool, distinguished self. When she was invited to sing and dance, she was the only performer to whom anyone paid attention. She was assisted by Sadaharu, who gave his own number, a modern dance piece choreographed for him by Béjart, based on a rather obscure version of the Narcissus legend, in which Echo was a handsome, slender drummer making wonderfully rhythmical echoes, while his 'best friend' played plangent notes on a Noh orchestra fife.

Hideki, always gracious and charming, made the rounds, saying goodbye to all his friends. He had never looked more beautiful. As he kissed the Major and Lorelei lightly on the brow, he murmured, with an attractive lisp, 'Thayonara. . . .'

Lorelei always wondered how Hideki could be both so sexy and sexless. It was an art. He looked so frail, so childlike, she had a sudden longing to mother him. He was a little waif in an enormous wig stuck with what looked like designer chopsticks and all kinds of pretty, dangling gewgaws – sprays of artificial wisteria, tiny gilded heads of rice, and indescribable doodahs that winked and tinkled to the movements of the head on the delicate neck.

She was perhaps the only one to feel real sadness at this parting, and tears – carefully controlled in order not to make her mascara run – came to her violet, pansy eyes as he waved and bowed his adieus.

Hilary's eyes were dry, but there was a look of unusual seriousness on his pancaked wrinkles. He alone knew that they would never be seeing beautiful Hideki again. The demure *onnagata* had seized the opportunity to go to the United States in order to escape the humiliation of having to die of Aids in gossip-plagued, shutterbug-infested Japan.

Now Hilary was trying to count the numbers of men – and women – he knew had been to bed with Hideki. He, fortunately, was not one of that number. But he soon lost count.

※18 : Flashback

※One of the reasons why Hideki/Fumiko had decided to go abroad for a while was the fact that his friend Major Hilary Sitfast had lost the manila envelope of important papers Hideki had left for him secretly in the toilet of the Russian coffee shop in Kanda.

Hideki was afraid of dangerous consequences, if the loss should be discovered by certain authorities like the secret police and the Ministry of Education. The Ministry had powers of life and death over the entire Japanese population. It could make or break a person's life. The slightest hint of an indiscretion was enough to exile you to social Siberias and cultural gulags worse than anything in dissident Soviet writers' tediously monolithic doorstoppers. So it was better not to make waves in Japan.

But the Major had not really lost the envelope. It had been stolen. Stolen by a disgruntled young man, a part-time waiter and full-time spy who worked at the Russian coffee shop – stolen by Kenji, whom the Major had badly misjudged. He had thought him a typical Japanese drifter, not switched on at all, someone close to imbecility. Attractive, in a pallid, constipated-looking way, and with a strokeable bottom, but, like most of the boys Major Sitfast picked up, deadly boring, and good only for twenty minutes or so between the sheets. Whenever the Major thought of the Japanese as 'aliens' or 'visitors from another planet', he thought of boys like Kenji, apparently aimless bodies from outer space, without will or wisdom, and only 'one of us' in the most elementary sexual sense.

Kenji, after performing rather listlessly in bed, and responding to Hilary's blandishments and allurements with well-practised groans and gasps, but disappointingly producing no satisfactory erection – always a dangerous sign, the Major knew – had shown himself to be in no hurry to get dressed and be packed off home in a taxi. The Major preferred to sleep alone after a bout of unsatisfactory sex. He had just wanted to get rid of this turgid youth and had no desire to see him again.

His pallid flesh was ornamented by several tattooed chrysanthemums arranged round a figure of Kwan-yin, Goddess of Mercy. Hilary shuddered at this grotesque example of *yakuza* folk-art.

Hilary, in a crimson Chinese silk dressing-gown and black silk pyjamas, had already laid a ten thousand yen note on the pillow beside Kenji's ominously sleepy-looking head, and given the boy a good shake. But Kenji still lay there, stark naked. The Major looked at him in distaste: how could he ever have gone to bed with that useless lump? It was a bad sign, he knew only too well, when short-time boys overstayed their welcome and refused to go home. It could mean only one thing: Kenji wanted more money. And the Major did not think he was worth it and was determined not to give it to him. Was he a part-time *yakuza* hooligan? 'One of those classic situations,' the Major sighed to himself.

Kenji lay back among the pillows, staring at Hilary with slightly crossed eyes, which now had a mean gleam in their tiny depths – like piss-holes in the snow, Hilary thought. And not only his face but his whole body seemed to have grown very sallow. There was resentment in every line of his undeveloped body. Even the naïve tones of his tattoos seemed to be turning rancid.

'Come on, Kenji, get up! I must sleep. I have to go to work early tomorrow.'

As Kenji made no move, except to scratch his pubic hair where the dew of the Major's useless sperm still glittered, Hilary attempted a final ploy. 'All right!' he cried as grimly as he was able. 'I'm going to get my friends from next door. If you don't get out of here in five minutes, I'll have you thrown out on your bare ass.' And he stormed out of the bedroom and down the stairs and into the street. There he hid behind his neighbour's fence and watched to see what would happen. To his satisfaction, he saw Kenji come out, fully clothed, and run away towards the Ginza to get a taxi. The Major smiled to himself: 'It always works.'

It was a chilly night in late November, so he at once went back to bed. The ten thousand yen note had gone, to Hilary's satisfaction. But the next morning he found that something else had gone: the manila envelope.

✻ 19 : Getting the Picture

✻ After living for so many years in Japan, and not just in Tokyo, Major Hilary Sitfast could still not come to terms with her inhabitants. Their faces remained inscrutable, their bodies often badly proportioned, their manners – despite their vaunted politeness in given situations – usually execrable.

He heaved yet another sigh as he was bundled into another packed commuter train. Finding himself jammed up against a couple of pickles-smelling housewives, he turned his gaze upon the other nearby occupants of the crammed space in which he found himself. The faces of the men were blank, the women betrayed a veiled curiosity. Among those fortunate enough to have found a seat he could discern not a single pleasant-looking face. There were some young students and older children sitting down, pretending to sleep so that they would not have to give up their seats to the old and infirm straphangers in front of them. The children were trained by their pushy mothers to shove their way into trains and buses and to bag seats for themselves and parents. The Major believed this kind of action was simply the result of the small area of living space allotted to each person in Japan. Bagging a train or bus seat was an assertion of territorial rights rather than impoliteness. That the Japanese did live in 'rabbit hutches' was for the most part undeniable; yet he had known people in America and Europe who lived in only one small hotel room or in a diminutive caravan – no one thought of calling such accommodations 'rabbit hutches', though they were smaller than the average Japanese apartment.

Among those who were awake on the seats during this afternoon rush-hour, the males were reading newspapers or comic books, the girls held paperbacks. It was considered unfeminine for girls to read newspapers. Their slim paperbacks were apparently cheap love stories and thrillers. Agatha Christie was very popular. Once again the Major marvelled at the ability of the Japanese of all ages to fall asleep anywhere at any time of the day. Trains were always places for sleep, but the sleepers always seemed to wake up in time to get off at the stop they wanted. Presumably the conductor's strident, ear-piercing tones over the maladjusted intercom worked subconsciously on their sleeping minds as he rattled off the names, not only of the next station but of the station after that.

Looking up at the many small, hanging advertisements, the Major saw one of Lorelei advertising a women's fashion magazine. She was dressed in expensive furs and appeared to be naked underneath. He was on his way to meet her in the Hilton coffee shop, which was quite near her new luxury apartment.

As usual, she was late. He ordered a 'remon tea' from the tall, skinny waiter in his sad-sack uniform. Like so many youths nowadays, he appeared to have no bottom and looked as if he had been force-fed and brought to callow maturity under artificial conditions, like out-of-season asparagus. Gazing around him, he noticed that nearly all the waiters had this overgrown, pallid, unhealthy look. You rarely saw an attractive face or figure these days. Hilary was reminded of one of the reasons why that awful bitch Virginia Woolf had committed suicide – she could no longer stand the sight of people's faces. Japanese faces did not have enough character to be called 'ugly' – they were simply plain and expressionless. Just as the Americans chew gum in order to give their features a certain masklike control, so the Japanese favoured eyeglasses and tinted goggles to make them look in complete charge of their emotions.

Lorelei came sauntering towards his table, all in black, like most of the young people, but with a large white-and-grey cloth badge over her left breast, printed with some indecipherable Janglish message. Her blonde hair had been frizzed out in a style that Hilary associated with loose women and low-class sluts. It gave him goose-pimples just to look at it.

'Konnichi-wa,' said the Major in greeting. Her hair looked
as if it might be swarming with lice. Glenn Close had a lot to
answer for.

'Oh, for fuck's sake, less of the conversational Japanese!'
growled Lorelei. 'Let's speak the Queen's English for a change.
I've been bowing and smiling all day long until I feel my back
is breaking, and my face has a permanent ache. I've had to take
off my shoes and kneel on the floor about twenty times, and my
knees are skinned, my ankles starting to grow calluses. Order
me a vodka tonic.'

Her first sip of the drink seemed to calm her down a little,
and she smiled wearily at the Major.

'Still no luck with the men?' he asked her.

'They all seem to back away as soon as they see me.'

'It's not your fault, love, it's theirs. They're afraid of getting
involved with a foreigner. To them, we always spell trouble.
We're a nuisance, really. We're creatures from outer space to
them.'

'Thanks for the information. But *they're* the ones from
another planet.'

'Can't you find some nice all-American boy?'

'They're all married, or Mormons on conversion trips, or
engaged to honey-buns back in the States, or studying to
become Zen priests, or moving on to China or the South Seas.
Or gay. Most of them seem to be gay.'

She gave Hilary a sidelong, apologetic look from under her
furry eyelashes. The areas under her eyes had a pinkish,
bruised appearance, while her lids were daubed with some
kind of blue-green fluorescent eye-shadow that gave her a
basilisk balefulness whenever she blinked. Today she had
painted her eyelashes the same fluorescent colour as her lids,
and she looked positively alarming. No wonder men steered
away from her, thought the Major.

He produced a recent issue of *HoKus PoKus* magazine,
and opened it at a page entitled 'Expo'. It was a full-page
photograph of a well-built and good-looking young Japanese
male in rugger shirt and shorts. He had obviously just emerged
from a scrum, and looked dishevelled and half mad. But the
feature the sneak photographer had focused on was something

that would never be seen in a Western weekly magazine: his
prick was hanging out of the front of his abbreviated shorts.
He seemed totally unaware of this, and was staring innocently
at the camera, or rather in the direction of its telescopic lens.
There was no name, no explanation.

'Good God!' Lorelei exclaimed. 'How dare they print a thing
like that?'

'It's a very nice thing,' murmured Hilary. 'I wouldn't mind
having my uvula round that lump of manly muscle.'

'But Hilary! It's obscene. It's unfair to expose an innocent
youth like that!'

'That's Japan for you. No privacy. Photographers and TV
crews interpret democracy as complete freedom to penetrate
the private lives – and the homes and offices – of anyone.
This is a throw-away society, and the throw-aways are people,
too, and their reputations. The damned camera is one of the
most evil inventions of our times. Especially in the hands of
witless Japanese photographers, who'll stop at nothing to get
a sexy or scandalous shot. They even have infra-red cameras
for photographing courting couples, gays and peeping Toms
in the parks and movies. It gives cameramen immense power,
because they know they can sell hot shots anywhere in Japan
– though nowhere in the rest of the civilized world would they
be allowed to publish a picture like this one, without fear of
prosecution. Japanese cameramen are the real dictators of
people's lives in this land.'

'I must say, he does look attractive. Quite a noble face.
It's the face that always attracts me first,' Lorelei explained.
'Perhaps that's why I've met no Japanese men I want to go
to bed with. This young rugger tough's face, and that mop of
thick, straight black hair – I could go for him. Who is he, by
the way?'

'The live-in houseboy of our beloved enemy Sir Paul Pinker.'

'Do you mean to say that old queen gets his arthritic hands
on this kind of sexual equipment?' The penis, though not
aroused in the picture, was obviously capable of attaining
respectable proportions.

'I'm afraid so, dear. But Taro's not gay. My Hideki
managed to get into bed with him because Taro thought

Hideki was a girl. There was hell to pay when the truth
– and Hideki's miniature prick – came out. But he makes
himself available to Sir P because of the prestige of being
protected by one of the diplomatic set. There's money there
too, of course. Taro's not the sort of boy to let himself go for
nothing. And I've discovered a very interesting thing. Sir P
has written his graduation thesis for him, which could create
a nasty scandal. And he's obtained the questions for Taro's
final exams, though those are quite useless, really, without the
special answers composed by the Japanese professors. It's not
enough, in a Japanese exam, just to know the answers. You
have to know the answers the professors have written. If your
answers don't fit the standardized pattern, you lose marks,
and can easily be put out of the running for positions in the
top-flight companies like Nippon Steel, the Bank of Japan,
Mitsubishi, etcetera etcetera.'

'I see.'

The Major drew a long breath. 'So what I want you to do
is to get this Taro in your toils. Hideki told me he'd had no
experience of women, still a very common condition among
Japanese youths, so you'll have to use all your charms and
wiles and little ways.'

'But how do I meet him?'

'Easy. Here's how. . . .'

It was the maple-viewing season. And as the branches of
plastic red and yellow maple leaves rustled in the streets, in
a drear wind blown from the already snow-dusted peak of
Mount Fuji, Lorelei listened to the Major's plottings.

It made her feel distinctly nervous, all these mysteries.
Was. she succumbing to the jitters that eventually attacked
most foreign residents in Japan? She kept trying to fight
off an indefinable sense of menace, of insecurity that did
not come just from the knowledge that a major earthquake
might obliterate Tokyo's neon fairyland at any time. For
years now 'the Big Quake' had been due to strike. . . .
She had her basic survival kit all ready. But that was
not what was making her sleep badly at nights, racked
by sexual nightmares and horror memories of the past, the
recent past, and the present. At any moment she felt the

privacy of her life might be invaded – by pressmen, scandal
mag reporters, secret police. When she thought about it, she
realized she had only one real friend in Japan. – Major Hilary
Sitfast. She had no Japanese friends. That was what was so
frightening. It was as if she were gradually being excluded
from society.

✳ 20 : An Unsuccessful Interview

✳ *'Foreign bachelor requires live-in houseboy to change his records and do the flowers.'*

'Girl Friday wanted for newly arrived couple with six children. No heavy duties. Cook kept.'

Driver for embassy car. Must be able to speak some English and know the streets of Tokyo.

Lorelei was browsing among the notices pinned to the notice-board at the Overseas Writers' Club, a comfortable old-world establishment in Mejiro. She had arrived ostensibly to be interviewed by one of the amateur foreign ladies, usually wives of major Western company managers, who pick up a little pin-money scribbling inconsequential gossip or fashion puffs for the English language newspapers. For Lorelei was now 'hot news'.

But she was also going to meet Taro there. The Major had arranged for him to do a modelling assignment with her for *Tokyo Journal*, an up-market monthly devoted to culture, entertainment and travel.

Tall young foreign blonde hostesses wanted for Cabaret Peep Show. Must have working permit and blue eyes.

Lorelei shuddered. She had been through all that. Being pawed and guffawed over in expensive male clubs was not her idea of pleasure, and the money was not all that much. The madames took 50 per cent of your earnings, and withheld salary if you did not bring in new customers. She remembered the first such 'members' club' she had worked for, where middle-aged businessmen came to be fondled and petted like babies. She had to wear a nurse's uniform, undress the men, powder them and put them in nappies. Another well-known club was for tired businessmen who wanted to relax in feminine garments. And there had been the Club Sappho, where she had to submit to inspection of her private parts by the lesbian wives of gay foreign businessmen.

On one occasion she had been asked to give a talk at the Association for the Foreign Husbands of Japanese Wives. What problems they had with the education of their 'half'-children, with their mothers-in-law, with incestuous mates seducing their own sons and daughters! The experience had made Lorelei thankful she had always turned down the proposals of old but wealthy and influential tycoons. In Japan, wives were nearly always acquitted of murder if it was within the family. And she had no wish to be exposed in *HoKus PoKus* as she nipped out of a love hotel or into her lover's private apartment set aside for the 'second wife', as mistresses were often called.

Lorelei was once more dressed in black from top to toe. It was an almost ankle-length alpaca sheath worn over tight, black eelskin pants – the latest thing from Korea. Only her trade mark, the chandelier earrings, remained from her former costumings. By now she had been offered lots of ropes of expensive cultured pearls, and these she wore not round her neck but wrapped round the skin-fitting sleeves of her dress, with an almost Renaissance Venetian effect. And, in memory of her performance as Desdemona, she had thrown another rope of pearls round her piled-up blonde hair, in a kind of loose turban. Emerald-green fluorescent eye-shadow and eyelash tinting. Black lipstick, teeth also blackened in the old style. As she glanced at herself reflected in a full-length portrait of Prince Charles and Princess Diana, she realized how quickly she had changed her extravagantly high-coloured earlier style to conform with the prevailing blackness. The Major, too, had made the change, almost overnight, into suits of black, with a gold-rimmed monocle of black glass attached to a chain of jet beads. We are all in mourning for our lives now, thought Lorelei. Soon I think I must abandon these too-showy earrings. And, anyhow, they do weigh down my ear lobes so. Her ear-lobes, when she took off her earrings at night, sometimes stretched right down to her shoulders. It needed a good night's sleep to unstretch them.

Outside, in the late autumn street, teenage girls were pursuing black men, to go with their black outfits. Black American soldiers and airmen from the bases round Tokyo were in great demand with clamouring teenagers, not always girls. The blacks had it made; they could take their pick. But they never picked Lorelei.

*　*　*

The interview with Gertie Gabble had not been a success. The ageing English columnist, a Tory Party member to the core, and a staunch supporter of the British matriarchy, felt an immediate aversion to Lorelei's flippant replies to her carefully studied questions.

'I've heard you're quite a dab hand at interior decorating,' she began condescendingly. 'I'm sure my readers would love to hear some of your ideas on how to "dress up" a rather cramped apartment, the sort that most of us have to live in here.'

'Dreary dog kennels,' suggested Lorelei. 'That's what they are.'

There was an awkward silence. Gertie hardly felt she could print that. She was one of those loyal foreigners who believe they are unofficial ambassadors or representatives of their countries, in whatever outlandish part of the world they find themselves. 'Quite,' she remarked, with a hypocritical, 'diplomatic' smile which, because of her dentures, came out on a sly slant.

'One entire wall of my kitchen', began Lorelei, as Gertie scribbled inefficiently in longhand, 'is adorned with paste diamonds arranged in the shape of an inverted phallus.'

The scribbling stopped. 'Oh yes?' said Gertie brightly, or as brightly as she was able, considering the fact that she did not know what a phallus was, had never seen one, and certainly did not know how to spell one.

'One entire wall of my master bedroom is hung with my hair-nets of the world collection. I have a probably unique assortment of the things, in every shade and shape, from

every era and every civilization. It's so lightweight. It's easy
to pack and to carry around with me when I travel.'

'Hair-nets!' was all Gertie could reply, but she had started
scribbling again. What could be safer than hair-nets? 'And
in what way unique? As you know by now, "unique" is the
favourite Japanese English word. You hear it everywhere.
People are always getting "unique ideas" and so on . . .'

'Yes, and in a culture where anything can be "unique"
because some nobody says it is, nothing can be "unique"
any longer. My collection, however, really is unique, because
nobody else has ever thought of creating a hair-net museum,
as I have. My most precious items are a hair-net, apparently
constructed of rusty chicken-wire, which was said to have
belonged to one of the Pharaohs, and one, more like a snood,
and said to be woven from pubic hair, reputed to have belonged
to a sister of Sappho.'

After that, Gertie Gabble drew her interview to a close as
soon as it was decently possible. Her editor, a bamboozled
Japanese with almost no understanding of English, was
waiting, but without impatience, for her copy.

'Thank God she's gone,' sighed Lorelei, sinking into a brown
velvet sofa to await the arrival of the Major with Taro and the
photographer. The place seemed to be filling up in a decidedly
sinister way with members of the Society for Battered Foreign
Wives of Japanese, a crestfallen lot, dragging moronic children
after them.

Good heavens, thought Lorelei, watching them all trail
upstairs to their monthly meeting, a lecture on 'Japanese
Divorce – Its Perils and Its Pitfalls', by a leading American
feminist who wrote an advice column for *The Nippon News*
and gave 'professional guidance' to newly arrived foreign
ladies whose Japanese husbands had already lost interest in
them.

Then Lorelei's withered heart gave a sudden leap and began
to flower. For there, coming through the entrance on the heels
of the Major, was the most divine young man she had ever laid
eyes on, followed by an elderly female photographer and her
teenage girl assistants.

So this was the gorgeous Taro. . . .

He gave her a brusque, stiff little formal bow, and in her confusion she dropped him a curtsy. The photographer and her assistants giggled, but there was no reaction from Taro. He was gazing at her with cold, calculating lust that made her feel weak at the knees. Hilary, his introductions made, left on another of his mysterious business appointments. 'I leave you to it,' he whispered as he took his leave of her.

She felt she was being tossed to this moody-looking young lion. 'Just wait till they start shooting,' she begged Hilary. She was decidedly nervous.

Hilary gave an impatient sigh, looking at his Mickey Mouse wrist-watch.

✺21 : Castle of Love

✺The photo session took place at the Meiji Shrine. The woman photographer, a lugubrious Japanese lesbian dressed in droopy clerical grey jacket and slacks, kept ordering her terrified little assistants to do this and that. They scuttled about like mice in their boiler suits laden with a wealth of industrial zippers. But they had learnt the liberated woman's blank scowl from their nasty employer, who sneered at every mistake they made.

All this activity, and the strain of changing costumes several times, kept Lorelei and Taro apart after their first introduction by the Major, who left 'on business' after the shots had started going well. 'There's a wonderful chemistry between you two,' he quipped in his usual flippant tone. But he was serious, Lorelei could tell.

The clothes were nearly all in dark tones – sooty rust, violet and sinister green, but mostly in several shades of dull grey and dusty black. Lorelei wore them all with her customary flair. But Taro, who was doing modelling for the first time, had an awkwardness that was most attractive, and made a fine contrast to Lorelei's smooth professionalism. They wore similar clothes throughout – pants, jodhpurs, workmen's breeches, cloaks, ankle-length tunics over black tights. But for the final shots Taro had to change into his rugger togs. The striped yellow-and-orange shirt, with its white schoolboy collar, was like a blaze of sunshine in the wintry shrine precincts; but, as if to conform to the prevailing pattern, his very short shorts were of worn black cotton, very moulding. Dark-red socks covered his calves which, as in most Japanese men, were rather flat and thin. But those bulging thighs and beautifully rounded, hard buttocks were undeniably sexy and aggressively male. The front of his black shorts was softly gathered, but from time to time, as he bent or stretched in various manly poses, his sturdy young sexual equipment thrust itself against the straining cloth.

To quote Quentin Crisp, Lorelei thought to herself, you can tell his religion. The penis of Japanese males is usually bereft of any sizeable foreskin – something she regretted, for she loved dallying with a capacious prepuce.

The final shot was of a wedding scene, and for this they were transported to a nearby Christian church that had been constructed by a Victorian architect from Britain and had great charm. But the wedding dress was all in subtle tones of black lace and bedraggled net, while Taro was in grey and off-white. The photographer decided that their appearance in the porch of the church, as her assistants tossed handfuls of black confetti, was out of keeping, so they transferred to the steel, modern ecclesiastical edifice at Mejiro, just opposite the celebrated Chinzanso Restaurant. There the clothes fitted the stark concrete interior and the ribbed metal walls, blinding in a late winter sun. Some semblance of a marriage ceremony was arranged, using the services of a defrocked clergyman who had seduced too many Japanese choirboys in the vestry.

Though it was just an imitation service, as are most of those so-called 'Western weddings' in which the Japanese indulge just for show after the traditional shrine ceremony, Lorelei and Taro felt some curious current of fatal attraction passing between them. Like all Japanese men in such a situation, Taro preserved a wooden samurai exterior, which was a perfect foil for Lorelei's acrobatic spasms and sentimental swoonings under her long black veil trimmed with small pearl butterflies. She had the look of Santa Teresa di Gesù in ecstasy by Bernini in the Church of Santa Maria della Victoria in Rome. Taro, if he had but known it, could have posed naked for the exquisite classical Greek sculpture of the Sleeping Hermaphrodite in the same church, as he lay on the altar steps in a vaguely crucified attitude, wearing severe white tights under an open black tailcoat. To conform with regulations, his sexual organs were reduced to invisibility by the use of a restraining strap.

Then Taro, drawing himself up to his full height, which was not inconsiderable, leant smilingly over her in the attitude of

Bernini's rapturous Angel, but holding in his right hand a black, tightly rolled umbrella instead of a golden arrow of desire. The photographer had chosen the prop, insisting that it was 'more modern'.

The photo session over, they all retired to Chinzanso for an early dinner. The Japanese, like the characters in Jane Austen, often take dinner around four in the afternoon, in preparation for an evening's revels in cabarets, bars and saunas.

It was a Japanese meal of sukiyaki, which Lorelei disliked because of the horribly 'marbled' Kobe beef from which it was made. But Taro ate this rather luxurious and expensive dish with great relish. They all complimented Lorelei on her use of chopsticks, the most common conversational ploy used by Japanese when wishing to condescend to Westerners. (But they were shocked when, in Western-style restaurants, she suavely complimented them on their handling of knives, forks and spoons – did she think they were uncultivated country barbarians who knew the use only of chopsticks?) Lorelei groaned inwardly, as all Westerners do, when the Japanese praised her in this way. Actually, she found chopsticks easier to handle than Western cutlery, and even used them to eat spaghetti.

The scornful photographer and her assistants left, and Lorelei and Taro strolled through the gardens of Chinzanso. They knew they belonged together, but could find nothing to say. Almost without a word being spoken, they took a taxi to a love hotel in Shibuya. It stood in a narrow lane with a number of other similar establishments, and they all had the price lists of their rooms prominently displayed outside, with rates by the hour. It had a tony French name: Château d'Amour.

They entered separately, in case there were any *HoKus PoKus* investigative photographers around. Lorelei went in first and booked a room for one hour, with the possibility of extension. She paid the three thousand yen and took the key. After a few moments, Taro entered and was given the number of the room by the desk clerk, who was completely hidden except for his hands. Taro could hear his voice only.

It was the first time Taro had entered such an establishment, which was of the utmost respectability. Lorelei had visited several already, once or twice on photographic assignments for a porno magazine, at other times with lesbian acquaintances picked up in record shops and gay bars. But this was the first time she had been in a love hotel with a man. And Taro, she felt it in her very bones, was a real man. At last. . . .

The room was large and luxurious, much larger and much more luxurious than any ordinary Japanese apartment bedroom. The false windows had plush curtains of bitter orange, and the floor and ceiling were both covered with a deep-blue carpet sprinkled with silvery stars and – a topical touch – Halley's Comet. The huge circular bed was slightly tilted towards one wall, which was all pink-tinted mirror. The fur coverings had been removed in readiness by invisible hands, and the black satin sheets and pillows lay gleaming invitingly under rosy spotlights. At the side of the bed was a control panel with many switches – for music, perfume, video tapes of erotic dalliance, vibrators and sexual aids. Lorelei imagined they would not require those red leather dildos her lesbian lovers insisted on shoving into her orifices.

The bathroom, too, was all *calme, luxe et volupté*, carpeted all over in sunshine-yellow deep pile. Even the sides of the wide bath were carpeted. A machine in the ceiling softly hummed as it breathed hot, scented air over the enormous black towels and the cakes of soap realistically shaped and coloured to resemble the intimate parts of both sexes. Tall stained-glass windows, back-lighted, represented erotic versions of *The Tales of Mother Goose*. The shower had enough room for two persons, with adjustable jets playing in all directions.

It was in this shower-womb that Lorelei and Taro first embraced. They just stood ecstatically, silent and motionless, their arms around each other, as the shower nozzles nuzzled and stroked their nakedness. Just to be held in a man's arms, after all this time, was an emotional revelation for Lorelei, who felt her whole being brimming with unshed tears as Taro laid his lips lightly on hers, an almost chaste, boyish kiss, exchanged with open eyes. Taro's eyes were long, slanting up into his temples in a faunlike way. They were larger than most Japanese eyes, darkly liquid like treacle toffee balls, richly warm and sootily fringed. His eyebrows were very strong, bold and thick – always a good sign in a man, Lorelei knew.

But it was not necessary to look at Taro's luxuriant black eyebrows for confirmation. His prick had leapt into immediate turgescence as soon as he put his arms around her, and Lorelei could feel the reassurance of that pulsing hardness without the need of hands.

But she wanted to see it. They stepped out of the shower and she dried him carefully all over. Without exchanging a word, she made Taro stand in front of her and stroke his massive erection. He could hardly bear to touch it, for fear of ejaculating too soon. The last time Sir Paul had drained him had been only twenty-four hours ago, but he was already brimful of seed again, and longing to spend it.

'Don't touch!' Lorelei commanded, and he dropped his hands. Then, under the pressure of her stare, without any touch of her body, he felt his whole being burst spontaneously into a shuddering orgasm. They both gazed in awe as his jets of semen hit the stars in the carpeted ceiling.

'That was just for starters,' Lorelei told him, licking away the last crystalline droplets from those delicious little strawberry lips that pouted at the tip of his glans, which she gave a lingering wipe with her able tongue. Taro gave a deep groan as she engulfed the whole of his slowly detumescent flesh in her mouth heated by the spices and herbs of the sukiyaki. Then, hand in hand, like the Babes in the Wood, they walked towards their tilted black bed under its rosy spotlights, while *The Rite of Spring* by Igor Stravinsky played on the biosonic stereo and all the embracings and uncouplings of the Kama-sutra unfolded on the video screen.

They paralleled each posture and penetration on the screen. Having been relieved of his first flush of tempestuous passion, Taro could now devote his throbbing rod to prolonged foreplay, to which Lorelei responded with equal ecstasy, in a carezza that seemed to last for hours as they gazed at their reflections in the mirror, and in a mirror in the ceiling which was revealed as Lorelei pressed a certain button and the carpeting slid apart.

What they did not know was that the mirror on the wall opposite the bed and the one discovered in the ceiling were one-way looking-glasses, and that eager eyes were watching them from the other side.

But in their youthful bliss they would hardly have noticed if a crowd of spectators had thronged the room to observe climax after climax, hour after hour, until dawn began to pale the sky above the bath-house chimney-smoke and television antennae and spiders' webs of telephone cables under which Tokyo lay like a trapped, iridescent insect of flickering neon colours. A hectic red flush infused the mirror above the bed with sinister, darkening, spreading clouds.

Who had been watching their every movement through the one-way mirror? It was someone who was in constant touch with the love hotel and who waited impatiently at home every evening hoping for a call to tell him whenever an especially choice couple had booked into the Kama-sutra Suite. He had to pay highly for the privilege, too. And he had invited three guests.

Early next morning, Taro was the first to leave the Château d'Amour, and a few minutes later Lorelei, on stopping at the entrance to pay the bill for all the extra hours all the extra hours, was puzzled to hear the invisible clerk assure her that they had already been paid for. . . .

But she was too much afloat on the scented clouds of romance to bother about solving mysteries. As she ran after Taro, now waiting moodily for her at the corner, her mind was filled only with her night of love and, curiously enough, with the image of her lover's navel, which was so deep and tasted so bitter. She was expecting him to kiss her goodbye. But he just turned on his heel and left her without a word. He had played his part in the plot, a plot so senseless and intricate it took on the aura of an almost religious mystery.

✿22 : The Peter No-Pan Bar

✿ 'Yes, dear, the temple's on the telephone,' sighed Major Hilary Sitfast.

Sir Paul Pinker nearly swooned. 'How too perfect,' he breathed. His great ambition was to become a Buddhist monk, 'if only for a day'. Now his wish seemed close to realization. 'I've heard', he said, biting into a cocaine-powdered cube of *crème de menthe* Turkish delight smuggled out of the Embassy shop, and admiring the subtle tones of the glaucous interior, 'that they're awfully *severe* with you, in these temple places.'

'Yes,' said the Major, 'if you like that sort of thing. And I believe you do. . . .'

Sir Paul wondered how the Major, an upstart, sissified, fake upper-class bounder, had discovered this hidden proclivity. After all, he had not been to a British public school, where the lash and the rod are part of a good boy's education for life. But he refrained from inquiring about the source of Hilary's information. 'Discipline,' he mused, in the good-humoured tone he used for the question-and-answer sessions at the end of his lectures on British ways. 'Discipline makes a change. Especially in Japan. A change, I mean, from all this oriental courtesy and politeness – just a mask of course, but traditional good manners. Those exchanges of conventional sentiments do oil the workings of society. Politeness is all.'

'And for an outspoken Westerner, that in itself can be the most exquisite torture.'

'The rack, my dear, the very rack.'

The Major had invited himself to meet Sir Paul Pinker, holding out the promise of 'an interesting proposition', something Sir P could never resist. Their meeting was taking place in a very 'contemporary' coffee shop, where the boys wore no panties under their frilly aprons and soothing music was piped into the chairs, which were also fitted with various vibrators to stimulate certain parts of the human anatomy. The coffee shop was called Bodysonic Boys. The Major had acted as 'technical consultant' for the décor, the English-language menus and the music. He had also had a hand in selecting the most suitable boys, and was proud of the fact that he had tested each one of them personally. Sir Paul was hoping for a few hints, and possibly an introduction. For his live-in-lover-houseboy Taro had left him, without a word of warning.

'These Buddhist priests are very male, very masterful, primed with cosmic energy and fanatical religious fervour, very sexy in their own self-renouncing way. Spartan chaps and all that.'

'So I've heard. The communal bath . . .'

'Those young disciples sometimes . . .'

'Oh, I say!'

'. . . have to endure . . .'

'Bliss! Bliss utter and utmost!' Sir P attracted a passing waiter by tapping his bare bottom. Pointing to the menu, he asked: 'What is Hot Sand?'

The boy, blushing all over, gabbled something in Japanese, leaving them none the wiser.

'I'll have a Hot Sand.'

'Reading between the Janglish lines, I'd say it was a toasted sandwich,' said the Major.

And so it proved to be.

'I rather go for that darling stocky boy with the pink frilly apron. You can see he has quite a bump in front. And the behind, though hairy, is cute.'

'Your style, dear, is becoming a trifle camp for one in such an official position. But I believe you have diplomatic immunity, whatever happens.'

'Quite true, so I do as I please. Anyhow, what matters it here? These people don't understand camp talk. They wouldn't know if it was Wednesday or Piccadilly. They're in a world of their own. Out of *this* world, anyhow.'

He gazed listlessly out of the black-curtained windows at the floods of Japanese riding by on scooters with curious Janglish names like 'Try' and 'Poppo' and 'Poet' and 'Because' and

'And'. Now why should anyone want to give that kind of
name to a Yamaha scooter? It was all too bewildering for
words. As so often in Tokyo, he felt he was lost and drowning
in the incomprehensibly banal. On the other side of the street
the junk-food rotundities of Colonel Sanders had been clad
in outsize Father Kissmess robes. Next door, a bank had a
flashing sign saying *Shocking Xmas*. Sir Paul felt thankful that
he had another Britisher to keep him company in the chaos,
even though the Major, of course, was not quite 'one of us'.

Despite his sillinesses and affectations, the Major was a
pretty sharp character, and always a pleasure to meet and
talk to. He was quite a mine of information about the most
diverse matters, and had a great store of arcane knowledge
derived from reading and observation, though you would
never guess it to look at him, even when, as today, he was
wearing funereal black with a violet 'half-mourning' monocle.
The nice thing about him was his modesty. He was not
like those dreadful old 'Japan hands' who, as soon as a
newcomer arrives, dazzle him with displays of fluent, outdated
Japanese slang and knowledge of 'little restaurants and bars
where they usually don't let aliens in, but they know me,
and so. . . .' Then one finds the place full of foreigners, all
suffering from the same Japanalian delusion. But Sir Paul was
determined to pump the Major for all he was worth: 'May I
call you Hilary – such an androgynous name, and how it suits
you!'

'Do, dear.'

'Now tell me more.'

'Well, in the Hall of Meditation, they give you great whacks
over the shoulders with a wooden stick.'

'Bamboo?' Sir P hopefully suggested.

'Not usually, but it could probably be arranged.'

'Bliss, utter.'

'I would suggest you take along your own riding-crop or
switch.'

'Really, what *do* you take me for?'

'A minor character from Ronald Firbank.'

'Oh, you *naughty* . . .'

'You have such long, thin, purple lips.'

'It's rude to make personal remarks. That's what I'm always telling my Japanese boys. They love making innocent comments about my "high nose" and my "round eyes" or my "Buddha belly" and so on.'

'Yes, I know. They keep tugging at my curls to see if they're real.'

'And to think I was once the avant-garde hope of the public schools debating societies.'

'It is said that you once wrote a poem entirely in capital letters. And another as full of italics as a chapter in the Bible.'

'Yes, that was the beginning of my literary fame. And fame, I find, is the only consolation for old age. But it was, alas, only the beginning, and I seem to have been beginning ever since. They still call me the white hope of British public school poetry, whatever that may be.'

'It's certainly not cricket.'

'Though cricket often comes into it, as a sort of slice to silly mid-on missed by a muff of a fielder who then with an overthrow surprises the lonely long-stop spooning in the long grass of the boundary with a stableboy or a bored team member from the rival school.'

'Play up!'

'And up!'

'At Guards and up 'em!'

They had moved on to glasses of Sir Paul's speciality, Blue Gin. He seemed to be in a state of incipient inebriation.

'I do think I'm getting a little tiddly. Where *are* my lecture notes? I have to do Yeats's 'A Prayer for My Daughter' at the YMCA – alas, not the hotbed of vice it used to be in the fifties – and last time I did it Miss Uttoxeter got all the pages mixed up, and nobody noticed. In fact, the last two verses were missing and I didn't know it myself. There was an air of intellectual fog in the audience. The BCS doesn't allow one the use of scent. If one is found out using so much as a wicked fairy godmother's dab of degenerate dew, one is banished at once.'

'Where to?'

'England. London. Rabies Street. Where the poor colonial students and the jaundiced Japanese sit in the waiting-room-cum-library with bated breath, reverently copying out page

after page of the *Cambridge History of Eng. Lit.* and handling
the *New Statesman* as if every word in it were Holy Writ.'

'Poor misguided darlings.'

'And not so much as a passing grope under the table. All the
English staff hate each other's guts, always doing one another
down in some way, consumed with perfectly rabid ambitions to
be appointed to Kuala Lumpur or Cairo or some such squalid
place. Dog does not eat dog, they say, but in Rabies Street
bitch *does* eat bitch.'

'To change the subject for a moment, Sir Paul. I believe you
are acquainted with a certain young man named Kenji?'

There was a speaking silence.

'And that he brought you certain papers in a large manila
envelope in exchange for a very large sum of money and a
forged Australian passport?'

Silence.

'Those papers were stolen by him from my apartment.'

'Oh.'

'And they contain not just the final examination questions,
but also – and most importantly – the answers.'

'I was just trying to help Taro . . .'

'Who has left you.'

'Do you happen to know where he is?'

'By now, I guess, with Lorelei Thrillingly. They're besotted
with one another.'

'And so. . . .'

At that moment an overpoweringly handsome black chauffeur wearing sherbet-mauve livery and a peroxided moustache
came in, carrying a whip of palest lemon-yellow silk floss. He
bowed as he handed it to Sir P. 'The limousine is waiting, sir,'
he announced threateningly.

He was parked illegally, but the Diplomatic Corps licence
plate always excused a multitude of misdemeanours, some of
them unmentionable in decent society.

'I'll be with you in a moment, Earl darling.'

The chauffeur left, his muscular breeches ogled by all the
no-pan waiters. Illegitimate son of a Japanese bar-girl and a
black GI, he was what the Japanese, with crisp insensitivity
to English, call a 'half'.

'I have to pick up some stuff from the Aix-en-Provence Gourmet Vegetable and Fruit Emporium. Would you care to accompany us? Fruits to the fruits and all that. . . .'

With a braying laugh, the sort we are told indicates a vacant mind, he swished out, flicking the bare bottoms of the boys in a perfect snowstorm of flailing floss. The Major followed.

'I'm afraid he's going to whip me down the back stairs and right out into Aoyama-dori, stark naked,' simpered Sir P. 'Thank God I left my corsets off.'

The Major smiled obediently at these sallies, privately patting himself under the left armpit to make sure he had his mother-of-pearl pistol well concealed.

'To the YMCA, Earl, and step on the gas, dear.'

And they drove away, past the trendy boutiques filled with black fashions, the Mister Donuts, the McDonald's hamburger joints, their golden arches incongruously elevated against the crimson ceremonial arch of a shinto shrine. From time to time they passed what looked like an immense green mosquito-net spread all over a vacant lot and rising to the height of several storeys – a golf driving range where hundreds of men were practising shots against black-and-white targets hung high up in the dusty green netting. Somehow the sight seemed to the Major like a symbol of present-day Japan: an insect-trap, in which a helpless nation struggled and played, waiting for the exterminating gases of some more virile enemy.

✺23 : Poor Lorelei!

✺'And who, may I ask, is likely to be present at such a do?' Lorelei inquired, soaping her navel, which had the appearance of a button chrysanthemum. She was being interviewed in her bath – that classical journalistic cliché – by Gertie Gabble, who was all eyes as well as ears.

Gertie glowed proudly at the question and, adjusting her brassière with a curious rubbing motion, replied: 'Well of course all the ladies of the Embassy set.' No tone could have been more reassuring. 'And I always cover our "meets", as our American friends call them. They are so refreshingly outspoken,' she added with a delicious shudder, poking her wig with the point of her ball-pen. 'They *will* call a spade a spade, even when it's a rake.'

A small gale of dyspeptic, ladylike merriment followed this inept remark, to show it was off the record – not that Lorelei had any intention of recording it. After her night of passion, she was still too much up in the clouds. 'I use a diamond-studded rake for my little garden,' she cooed, combing her abundant pubic hair with the item in question, while Gertie eagerly scribbled down the information.

Lorelei heaved a magnum of pink champagne out of the ice-bucket held by a small, kneeling Japanese serving-woman in the costume of the Heian period.

'Of course our group has serious aims as well as social,' burbled Miss Gabble, waving aside a flute of the sparkling, rose-tinted liquid. 'We do try to keep up standards here. Scholarships for underprivileged boys, for example, sewing outfits for the girls, sexual initiation for promising young artists.'

'Standards?' queried Lorelei, groping for her glass, which had got lost somewhere in her bubble bath. 'Junko,' she commanded her maid, 'bring me a clean glass and a fresh bottle.'

The little maid scurried across the bathroom floor on her knees, in imitation of certain moments in 'Grand Kabuki', as it was erroneously billed in *The Nippon News*. She produced a new glass from a gauzy kimono printed provocatively with aggressively 'male' irises. Then she rose from her aching knees in search of a fresh bottle. She was intended to represent a Lady Murasaki with rather advanced ideas.

'Yes,' piped Gertie defiantly, her eyes on the diamond rake whose rounded handle was exploring regions out of sight. 'Standards.'

'Such as what?'

Gertie took a deep breath. 'Well, our great task in these parts of the world has been to bring British chintzes into Japanese life. You know, dear, *they*' – she nodded sideways with a wink at the Heian maid – 'don't understand chintzes. They don't see the beauty of brown, rose-patterned chintzes on a nice three-piece suite. So we have to fight, literally *fight*, for recognition of British chintzes. Despite our diplomatic pull, you wouldn't believe how obstinate the Ministry of Imports and Exports can be.'

Lorelei, bored almost to tears, began throwing liqueur chocolates at the ceiling, decorated with a reproduction of the Marcel Duchamp Mona Lisa, condensation dripping from the end of her disapproving nose and richly beading her moustache. Blackness was all. Not only in fashion. 'Surely a somewhat otiose labour of love,' she commented, taking unerring aim with a chocolate cacao liqueur at Mona's cleavage. Lorelei was already quite tipsy, and it was not yet tea-time. 'Always exaggerate,' she instructed an agape Gertie, in patent self-excuse, plying a fan of paper painted with an 'improper' haiku with an abnormal number of syllables, which began to dissolve in the perfumed (Ruined Temple Garden) waters of the bath. She was obviously not herself, which, strangely enough, was when she was always *most* herself.

Something rumbled.

'Was that me or the drain?' mused Lorelei, observing a flight of rather larger bubbles from the depths of the foam.

'Beg pardon,' Gertie Gabble sniffed, turning her head away slightly. (Really, the awful situations a nose for a story got you into!). She flushed, fixing as if in abstract distraction a boiled-looking eye on the rainbow ripples of piquant foam subsiding round Lorelei's emphantic bust.

'These bubbles tickle,' Lorelei giggled, rubbing her breasts with the frankness of a small child wiping its mouth after a social kiss. 'And these earrings – they tire me. Remove them, Junko.' Her voice had taken on the tones of Cleopatra preparing for the bite of the asp.

Junko reverently removed the dripping diamond chandeliers and laid them to dry on oblongs of hand-made paper.

'We Embassy ladies are doing everything within our power,' Gertie was gabbling on, 'as upholders of British decency and all that, to bring British chintzes to the Japanese people – chintz kimonos, chintz sashes, chintz Dorothy bags, chintz happi-coats, chintz tatami bindings, chintz *fundoshi* . . . everything chintz, chintz, chintz . . .'

'Stop, you're making me dizzy with your chintz this and chintz that,' moaned Lorelei. Just to pronounce the word 'chintz' gave her a splitting headache. 'It's perfectly egregious.' (She meant 'tiresome', but, once learnt, she could never resist the use of a *Times* crossword brain-twister, however inappropriate.) Life was turning grim indeed. 'I am in mourn-ing for my life,' she intoned, closing throbbing eyes. She kept having visions of how cruelly Taro had left her standing there at the corner of the love-hotel lane. She despised champagne as a terribly bourgeois drink, but it was the only thing that dulled the various kinds of pain now afflicting her body and her soul.

'Junko, take the champagne out of the cooler!' The Mumm from Meidi-ya American and European Provisions Emporium was bound to be in poor condition. It was a monumental flagon gaily bedecked with gold-threaded pink ribbon and reposing at an interesting tilt in the floral-patterned lavatory bowl, specially packed for the occasion with lavender-tinted ice-cubes.

Gertie Gabble opened her chops again to say something, and suddenly Lorelei felt she could not bear another minute of her company. 'How extenuating you are, you old bitch,'

she cried in a ferocious malapropism. 'Get the hell out of
here!'

'Well, if that's the way ... I must say ...' Gertie hissed,
bridling, as she scuttled out, dying to retail the spicier bits of
her interview to the ladies at the Club.

Lorelei heaved a sigh of relief.

'You should eat something, Madame,' suggested Junko.
'Food is good for a broken heart, they say.'

'Who says?'

'People say.'

'So what?'

'I can make you some Cup Noodle.'

'The very thought of that junk food makes me want to
puke.'

'Yes, Madame.'

'The very thought of that stupid name, too. It sounds as
if there was only one noodle in the cup. I keep telling
the manufacturers it should be "Cup Noodles", but they
don't take any notice. To the Japanese, English is just a
sales-promoting commodity that gives a superior cachet to
anything basically inferior. They couldn't care less about
correctness. The Japanese language is taking over English
wholesale and making it its own, with its own rules, its own
demented grammar and ridiculous spellings.'

Junko was silent after this outburst. She didn't really know
what Madame was getting so heated about. What did a few
words matter?

But there was some excuse for Lorelei's unusual savagery
and bitterness. A few days ago the TV news-reader had
po-facedly reported the deaths, in mysterious circumstances,
of a certain Major Hilary Sitfast and the eminent literary figure
from Britain, Sir Paul Pinker. They had been discovered with
their throats cut in a 'special room' with a two-way mirror
in the floor at the love hotel called Château d'Amour
in Ikebukuro. The police had investigated the case very
efficiently. Apparently these two very different pillars of
gaijin society had been involved in drug-running and had
been invited to the love hotel to witness the love-making of
Lorelei and Taro by an unnamed but very influential *yakuza*

boss to reward them for bringing in a new load of cocaine. But
Kenji, seeking revenge on both the foreigners, had also been
invited, unknown to Hilary and Sir P. He had been summoned
by the gangster boss to prove his worth as a *yakuza* apprentice
by committing his first murders. The boss had chosen that
pair of foreigners because he knew they had tried to swindle
him out of some of the ill-gotten gains – something a *yakuza*
could never forgive.

Taro, too, was in the gangster organization and had spied
upon Sir Paul. He had pretended to let himself be seduced by
Lorelei, intending to prove his worth to the boss by the murder
of the two foreigners. But he had been carried away by his own
pretence of love and Kenji had beaten him to it.

Furious after his night of bliss, Taro had dashed away from
Lorelei to Kenji's coffee shop, where he found the manila
envelope containing the exam answers in a secret hiding-place
known only to the two *yakuza* postulants.

Kenji had gone into hiding, but the secret police soon
found him and arrested him for the double murder. But
under interrogation Kenji revealed that he had Aids. The
police kept this quiet. No Japanese was supposed to have
this shameful disease of the blood. But he and Taro had
been lovers, brought together by Sir Paul, who had enjoyed
watching them and taking part in their amorous battles.

So Taro . . . and Lorelei, lovely Lorelei. The pretty spreading clouds of blood on the mirror in the ceiling would come back
to haunt them both.

Death is indeed like grass, a great leveller. Thus the two
enemies, arch rivals for the educational and cultural and sexual
domination of both *gaijin* and Japanese life in the capital, had
been reconciled, united in a grotesque and hideous death with
appropriate elements of erotic titillation, pornographic peeping
Tomism and the consumption of drugs, which in Japanese eyes
was the worst crime of all and the deepest disgrace.

And they had both died not knowing that they were already
infected with the poison of the century. They could not have
lived much longer in any case.

✳24 : Peace and Love

✳It was New Year. The Year of the Boar. Lorelei refrained from making unsuitable puns on the word. But it was indeed a more than usually boring time for her and for most foreigners.

Half the capital had left, by train, plane and boat, for home towns or foreign destinations. Hawaii was the favourite. Tokyo streets were strangely vacant. Offices and factories were all shut down for at least seven days. For *gaijin*, this period after the gruesomely commercial un-Christian revelry of Japanese Kissmess was the worst, the most lonely time of the year. All the stores were shut, and most of the restaurants. The only place where one could get a meal was in one of the hotels. For a moment, Lorelei considered the possibility of spending New Year in a room at the Vanity Fair. But she could not face the memories such a visit would bring. And she did not fancy facing the hordes of Japanese families and their offspring, spoiled silly with presents and money, and ruder than ever in their obstinate staring at foreign faces. Yes, at such a time, Japan was truly unbearable. Truly black.

But for the Japanese all was well and getting better all the time. The murders had been hushed up in the press, and even the scandal magazines had found it hard to get enough material to fill a double page.

One of the happiest persons at this time was Taro. He had got his hands on the answers to the exam questions, so a radiant future lay ahead of him when he graduated in March. It would be spring again, no longer black winter. The cherry blossoms would be blooming, and there would be the sake parties and loud singing and dancing under their silent domes of pink and white.

Lorelei was also looking towards the spring. It would be time to start life again. Let the Japanese go their own way, she thought, and she would go hers. That was the best way for *gaijin* and natives to live in harmony. Despite all the talk about 'internationalism', the Japanese were becoming more and more ingrown. They seemed to be returning to the closed society of the pre-Meiji period in the middle of the nineteenth century. There was no such thing now as an international and democratic way of life. It was every nation for itself. Sad but true.

After the Major's funeral, performed with Buddhist rites which she found almost unbearably moving – (how she had wept!) – Lorelei had been taken by distraught Sadaharu to Hilary's Ginza apartment, little more than a dark cubby-hole. It was the first time she had entered it. Hilary had never invited her there. Perhaps he was ashamed of its meanness.

Sadaharu had allowed her to take possession of the Major's collection of tinted monocles. Hilary, unknown to everyone, including Sadaharu himself, had made the boy his heir in a long-standing will. It became clear that this unlikely pair had loved one another deeply. Perhaps because there had been no sexual attraction whatever between them.

Sad became therefore the proprietor of the Cambridge English Academy. He was planning to introduce a course called 'English by Aerobics' for overweight and even obese girls (their numbers were increasing) wishing to learn the English words for the various parts of the body and at the same time shed a few kilos. But the Business English classes would continue. Sad was already recruiting new arrivals from the United States and Britain, 'fresh off the plane' and without much cash in their pockets, most of them with no qualifications at all. The place would never be the same again without the Major's scintillating if eccentric intellectual stimulus, his generosity with holidays and time off, and his loving leadership of promising orphans and other likely lads.

Not long after this funeral, Hideki's body was brought back from the States for cremation. The drummers' extended tour had been a great success, a sell-out, and the show had been invited to visit the People's Republic of China and the USSR. But Hideki, the elegant, beautiful and refined, would not be going with them. He had barely had strength to hold out until the end of the tour. The show's peculiar fascination for homosexuals of every bent filled him with bitterness. Now, gone were his brilliant costumes and accessories, and his body returned dressed all in white. His death created a great shock in Japan, where fortunately states of shock are very common and do not last for long, like earthquakes. But the press photographs of his weary, emaciated face, refulgent eyes and withered corpse were truly horrifying. He became one of the growing number of Aids victims in the Land of the Rising Sun.

Another, eventually, was Taro, at the start of a brilliant career, in which his *yakuza* connections were serving him well. He had been given a position at the Foreign Office, and already he was looked upon as a promising, rising politician. His *yakuza* bosses arranged his marriage and financed his new house. Too late he learnt that he was infected. His wife and child were infected too. But the whole thing was hushed up by the Ministry.

Not so the death from Aids of Lorelei. She made the front pages of all the newspapers for many weeks, and filled the pages of the scandal magazines for months on end. Every tiniest detail of her private life was nosed out and spread crudely before a gaping public. The growing sense of doom and menace she had felt had proved to be well founded. She was literally crucified by the Japanese press after her agonizing death. They had even invaded the hospital to film her dying moments. But then she was not a Japanese like Taro. She was only a *gaijin*. Just another of those crazy *gaijin* one sees on the Ginza.

☀ Epilogue : The East Is Extreme

☀ In tense, treacherous Tokyo, where the East is always at
its most extreme, the masses of pink cherry blossom had given
way to displays of 'male' irises. Then would come the seasons
of wisteria, azalea, peony and chrysanthemum. Whatever the
season, the blackness never relented: even amid the floral
festivities of Golden Week, the traditional kimono of New
Year, the rites of Children's Day, there was always a black
undercurrent. As the new Emperor's coronation drew near,
the police were out in full force, day and night, and there were
some harmless little bombs.

It was the merry month of May, when half the population
went on shopping sprees to Hong Kong or Hawaii. A high-
school girl won first prize in a nation-wide essay contest with
three hundred words on 'My Hobby Is Shopping'. A rising pop
philosopher invented the slogan 'I Shop, Therefore I Am'.

But there were dark reports of Russian submarines and
warships circling the islands of Japan: despite the diplomatic
visits of Schevardnadze and Gorbachev, perestroika and glas-
nost could not stretch as far as Tokyo. The Chinese, too, were
becoming less accommodating as they prepared to annex
Hong Kong; but the only worry of most Japanese was 'Will
we still be able to go shopping there in 1997?' No peace treaty
had ever been signed with the Russians after the Second World
War. They were still hanging on to the island of Sakhalin, just
a few miles away to the north of Cape Wakkanai in Hokkaido.
One got the impression that they, or the Chinese, could land
in Japan at any time, and no one would lift a hand to stop
them. The peace-loving Japanese would probably bow low and
welcome them with white flags and flower arrangements. It
would be a situation rather like that described by Maupassant
in 'Boule de suif', when the invading Prussians in Rouen were

tolerated and accepted because they were 'correct'. If the Russians landed in Japan, they would surely be quite correct too. They would be accepted as easily as the French for the most part accepted the Nazis, as the Japanese themselves accepted the American Occupation. It was now the Japanese who were the occupiers, not only of their own land but of large parts of the Western world, and without spilling a drop of blood.

Most Japanese now seemed incapable of being serious about learning foreign languages or reducing trade friction or revolutionizing their archaic educational system. There was a new fad afflicting both young and old: apathy. The intellectual magazines and even scandal weeklies like *HoKus PoKus* were swamped by essays and symposia featuring the latest local and foreign TV idols on the subject of 'The Age of Apathy'. The Japanese were content to discuss their contentment. Though they travelled abroad in their millions, they were becoming less and less international. Foreign travel served only to show how much more comfortable they could be in their own land, and increased their pride in it. Whether or not the pride was justified was something that never entered most people's heads. They were blinkered by a success that had come almost without trying, through the reduction of the imagination and the standardization of every aspect of human existence. Japan was forever the land of effects without causes.

So in the Age of Apathy any passing frivolity was always welcome, to take rigidly tutored minds off relentlessly limited responsibilities and minimal international obligations of 'We Japanese'. After the fads for the Papua New Guinean fringed lizard, which refused to raise its pretty frill; the disappointment with the cuddly koalas, which could inflict nasty bites and died of stress in city zoos; the excitement about Aids, which reduced the sex tours to Korea, the Philippines and Thailand; and the craze for pastel-tinted kittens – what new diversion could be created to keep people's minds off the real issues at stake? After all, million-dollar Van Goghs are in fairly limited supply. November came, with its chrysanthemum displays.

A slight diversion was caused by the visit of Prince Charles

and Lady Di to attend the 'coronation' of the new Emperor
Akihito. European royalty was always 'cute'. Even Queen
Elizabeth and Margaret Thatcher had been enthusiastically
welcomed, then immediately forgotten. In a land of earthquakes, short attention spans are inevitable. The police were
out in their thousands. Would the coronation delay the arrival
of the Beaujolais Nouveau? That was one of the main worries of
the common people, who had been brainwashed into revering
this cheap and nasty 'counter wine' palmed off on the Japanese
at exorbitant prices.

The royal couple, widely reported in the scandal mags to
be not on speaking terms, arrived in time for the Armistice
Day ceremony at the International Cemetery on the Bluff in
Yokohama. The entire staff of the Embassy and of the British
Cultural Association was present, each one wearing a drab
little artificial poppy. It was a brilliantly fine late autumn day,
and both the Prince and Princess lost no time in remarking how
nice it was to have good weather for the occasion. The Prince
was escorted by his guru, a minor novelist. A bespectacled
Japanese professor, who had published a computer study of
the frequency of the word 'and' in the novelist's works, rushed
forward, beaming, to greet him with the title of one of his better-
known works, which had been turned into a ghastly movie:
'Melly Kissmess Mister Rollins' was rather inappropriate,
but the guru accepted it with his usual inscrutable Zen calm,
carefully cultivated for the occasion.

The royal party passed the newly dug grave of Sir Paul
Pinker, where they saw a bright new lilac marble stone copied
from Oscar Wilde's monument in the Père Lachaise. It bore
the simple, chaste inscription *Homo in Omnibus*. The Cultural
Attaché noticed with a wince of disapproval that Sir Paul's
date of birth had been arranged to suggest that he had been
called away in the prime of youth, to give the impression that
he was one of those whom the gods loved and had therefore died
young. The grave was massed with black chrysanthemums. An
unusual feature of the monument was an electronically worked
scent spray which doused all those who approached the site
with Chanel's Egoiste on even days, and Flowers of Lethe on
odd days.

During the two-minute silence there was a sinister cawing of crows. But the reverent hush was suddenly broken by the apparition from behind the war memorial of Lorelei, all in black lamé, her deathly white mask of suffering slashed by sequined black lipstick. She had dyed her flaming blonde hair jet-black and had had a cosmetic surgical operation to insert an epicanthic fold in her eyes, giving them the authentic oriental look. She was bearing a placard on which was inscribed one of Major Hilary's last haiku:

> We refuse to wear
> the flower of forgetting
> on Remembrance Day.

The gun salutes rang out to mark the end of the two-minute silence. Turning to the Ambassadress, Lady Di asked in hushed tones: 'Isn't that. . . .' A pause. 'One seems to have seen her . . .'

'Yes, it is,' the Ambassadress hissed. She was world famous for that special hiss, used to reprimand the native help at Embassy receptions.

'She was once on that TV panel game with Charles and me.'

'A sad come-down for a promising actress, I'm afraid. She got taken up by the local queers, became what I believe is called a "fag hag" and was related to that simply dreadful bounder Hilary Sitfast, a person utterly beyond the pale. He died recently of that disgusting disease they all get. For some reason they refer to it as "Maids in the kitchen". That kind of *Galgenhumor* is quite beyond the rest of us.' She and her 'hubby', Sir Peter, had spent three dreary years in Vienna, and she took every opportunity to flourish her few words of German, pronounced with a marked Birmingham accent.

The professor, eyelashes flashing as relentlessly as his blindingly white teeth, sidled up to Prince Charles and asked: 'Is that the editorial or the royal "we" in the first line, Your Highness sir?'

The secret police drew near. The Ambassador waved them away.

The Prince turned to his guru with his celebrated raised-eyebrows, quizzical expression that had made him beloved by millions of Britishers.

'What's he on about?'

'They like to check subtle points of English grammar with native speakers – from the horse's mouth, as it were.'

'I suppose that's what they call a haiku?'

'Yes, I'm afraid so – seventeen syllables plus a season word and all that.'

The secret police were grinning, doubling in their fingers to count.

The royal party moved slowly towards the gates, where a small crowd of hired schoolchildren with Rising Sun flags were waiting to scream and wave.

'I hear the new Emperor is a perfect dear,' Lady Diana remarked conversationally, casting a regulation smile at the kids.

'Yes, and *she's* such a darling,' the Ambassadress agreed.

'I believe there is a new name for the era – the Age of Apathy was what I saw in *The Sunday Times*.'

The Ambassadress tittered. 'Actually, it's "Heisei".'

'Hay-say,' the Ambassadress spelled out conscientiously. It was something she had had to explain already several hundred times to 'visiting firemen'.

The Prince had overheard this snippet. 'Sounds like something from the lips of Billy Bunter,' he drawled wittily. "Hay say, you chaps" and all that.'

'Or possibly P.G. Wodehouse,' the guru suggested.

'What does the damn thing mean, anyway?' the Prince demanded in one of his sudden fits of impatience.

'Something like "Peace and Love", I believe, the Ambassador replied, fending off the Japanese professor who was all ready to give a lecture on the new name's significance.

'How sententious!' Lady Di remarked.

'They love those abstract words, you know,' the guru explained before they all inserted themselves into their official cars. 'I suppose it's because at bottom they're so pragmatic, they like to cover up with a bit of metaphysics.'

'It's all Zen to me,' groaned the Prince as they drove away

past the Gland Hotel and through the streets of Chinatown already gaudy with Christmas decorations and slogans like *My Hobby Is Shopping* and *Wholly X, mas* and *Missis Christmas Shock*. All along the streets were cherry-red public telephones outside the shops, where people were telephoning, bowing again and again to the invisible interlocutor. Everybody stopped to wave and shout 'Bye-bye', covering their mouths politely to hide their laughter at the audacity they had shown in using English, that comical tongue. For after all, the Royals were just *gaijin*. And *gaijin* are always good for a laugh in this temporary land, where the best things are passing shadows in a floating world of fleeting illusions. That is why *gaijin* are so popular. Like disposable pets, they never stay for very long, and there are always newer and more amusing ones to take the places of those who have become too familiar, too much at home.

Back in the cemetery, Lorelei was drenching herself in Flowers of Lethe. She would not be much longer for this world. She picked one of the black chrysanthemums from Sir Paul's grave, stuck it in her hair and wandered to the gates, where no one took any notice of her as she drove away in her chauffeured Alfa-Romeo. The driver had those deliriously high cheekbones that always used to turn her on. But now, she realized sadly, she could observe them with total equanimity. Even those long, mysterious, dark eyes sloping up into the creamy temples. . . . The secret police were everywhere.

She composed herself for sleep, and did not wake up until the car got held up in a traffic jam in that shopping paradise of sordid cuteness, the Ginza.

The police were trying to control zigzagging ranks of revolutionary students chanting unintelligible slogans against the Government, the imperial family, the extensions to Narita International Airport. Lorelei gazed at the jigging youths in their white helmets and white towels covering all but their eyes, and thought: What a waste of energy. They should all be in bed, working off steam in orgies of sex. They're all suffering from sexual frustration, poor things. There was a time when I could have put them right. But that's all in the past now. Japan seems to have become neutered by success.

But her meditations were suddenly interrupted by an attack of feverish sickness. She vomited picturesquely all over her black lamé gown, splattering Major Hilary Sitfast's last haiku. The insipid NHK radio programme was playing what the announcers called 'ballock music'. Before Lorelei finally passed out, a tender thought flashed through her collapsing brain: I'm living proof that to err is human.